"Lie with me,"

she asked again, and again he neither left nor consented. Hypnotized, he stood.

Danielle's back was turned to the land and her face was turned to Seth, who stood between her and the sea. She unfastened the tiny, old-fashioned buttons at her throat.

"Lie with me," she whispered again, while she held the fabric of her nightgown at her breast.

"No," he said harshly.

She let the gown slip away.

With a groan, Seth reached for her, and with reason destroyed he swept her forcefully into his arms. Caution flung aside, all thought flung aside, he carried his naked temptress through the night.

ABRA TAYLOR

was born in India, where her father, a doctor of tropical medicine, treated both maharajahs and British viceroys. Exposed to exotic places and unusual people from an early age, she developed an active imagination and soon turned to writing. The author of numerous romances, she is today a beloved storyteller, whose books are sought after by fans world wide.

Dear Reader:

Romance readers have been enthusiastic about Silhouette Special Editions for years. And that's not by accident: Special Editions were the first of their kind and continue to feature realistic stories with heightened romantic tension.

The longer stories, sophisticated style, greater sensual detail and variety that made Special Editions popular are the same elements that will make you want to read book after book.

We hope that you enjoy this Special Edition today, and will enjoy many more.

The Editors at Silhouette Books

ABRA TAYLOR
Sea Spell

Silhouette Special Edition
Published by Silhouette Books New York
America's Publisher of Contemporary Romance

SILHOUETTE BOOKS, a Division of Simon & Schuster, Inc.
1230 Avenue of the Americas, New York, N.Y. 10020

ISBN: 0-671-53692-3

First Silhouette Books printing September, 1984

10 9 8 7 6 5 4 3 2 1

Map by Ray Lundgren

Books by Abra Taylor

Silhouette Special Edition

Pocket Books

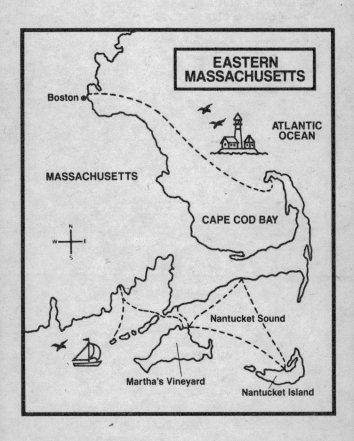

Chapter One

The faint cry of a sea gull pierced the air. In the darkened room the man began to stir drowsily. The one sheet that covered him had become inadequate in the night chill. Groggy with sleep, he rolled sideways in the oversize bed, reaching out automatically for the warmth of a woman's body. When his hand encountered nothing but empty bed, he muttered a soft curse and came awake enough to remember that he was on Nantucket and temporarily womanless.

Still only part awakened, he sat up, and in the darkness started to fumble for the blanket he'd thrown to his feet the night before. Sleeping naked, when no one shared his bed, had its disadvantages.

It was then that he heard the sea gull repeating its call. Night? Good God, no; it must be morning. Ruefully, he realized that his sea-senses must have become somewhat dulled by the last few years of drivingly hard desk work. There had been a time when he wouldn't have slept past dawn.

Normally, because he liked to wake to the sun, the flutter of sheer curtains would have admitted streams of light, but as it had been long past dark when he'd arrived at East Widow, the outside storm shutters were still tightly closed. After the long day's sail over to Nantucket, and especially after being caught in a line squall, he'd been too damn exhausted to do more than fling a single window open before falling into bed. In the dark he hadn't been able to locate all the latches for the outer shutters, anyway; the high wind had knocked out the electricity.

Yawning, he fumbled at the bedside table until he located a light switch. It worked. The electricity was back on, thank God. He flung back the sheet and rolled out of bed. Moments later he was at the window, easily finding the hooks that had eluded him the night before. He flung open the shutters and grinned to see the good, clean morning. The brief storm had washed the world so that the cove of Three Widows shone like new. Gold sun, silver sand dunes, lightly ruffled blue sea stretching as far as the imagination. He inhaled deeply, feeling the tang of salt air in his lungs, the tremble of a medallion against the golden fuzz on his chest.

Enjoying himself hugely, he stretched his large muscular body, feeling a few aches from the rigorous exercise of the previous day—enjoying even those aches, because they gave him a sharp sense of aliveness. He was a man who enjoyed life as well as women, and he felt he hadn't been enjoying enough of either for the past few years. He'd been too damn occupied with work.

From small clues—the activity of the gulls, the roll of the surf, the length of spidery shadows cast by clumps of poverty grass on the high dunes close to East Widow—he could tell it wasn't much past dawn. The coolness of the air confirmed it, and so did a glance at his watch. The sun had risen only minutes before.

The water called to him, as it always did. "Damn," he muttered, remembering that he'd been unable to find a bathing suit when throwing his clothes together for the trip. Usually he didn't have to pack for himself, but his Man Friday had been off on other errands.

A skinny dip, then? Well, why not? There should be time before the occupants of the two other houses woke. The two old sisters who lived in West Widow must be pushing ninety, anyway; if their eyesight was still sharp enough to see anything, it would give their gossiping tongues a good chance to wag.

Middle Widow—center of the Three Widows, as the large identical homes in the cove were locally known—was usually rented out, although in June the summer tenants probably wouldn't have arrived. And even if they had, renters were generally city folk who didn't wake at the crack of dawn.

Whistling softly between his teeth, the man made his way to the bathroom adjoining the master bedroom and found a thick white towel. Slinging it neatly around his lean, powerful hips, he made his way down the great curved stairs. The study of East Widow, like the studies of all of the Three Widows, opened directly onto a terrace overlooking the dunes. He was about to step through the door when he saw, first with a flash of disappointment, that another early riser had beaten him to the sea.

It certainly wasn't one of the old sisters from West Widow. Not with that shape. Not with that hair. As his appreciation grew, his disappointment faded. Whoever she was, she had as much right as he to displace the sea water. And as far as he could see from this distance, she was about to displace it very nicely indeed. He'd always had a weakness for tall, slender women who stood proudly and carried that particular shade of rich auburn on their heads.

When he walked out onto his terrace, she didn't turn. With the sounds of surf and sea wind in her ears, she hadn't heard the faint clatter of shuttered doors opening behind her.

With the periphery of his mind, he noted that Middle Widow wasn't boarded up. The window shutters stood open against the weathered silver shingle of the house. But he didn't actually look sideways to inspect the building; he kept his eyes trained on the auburn-haired woman who must be the new tenant.

She was standing at the water's edge, wearing an oversize T-shirt—a man's T-shirt, from the look of it. It was hard to be sure, but from the way it clung, he idly wondered if she wore nothing underneath. Curious and temporarily unconscious of his own state of semi-dress, he came to a halt just outside his door. He stood with a faint frown tugging at the edge of his mouth, waiting to see if she planned to take off her garment. If she did, he didn't intend to embarrass her; he would simply vanish back into the house.

She took a few steps into the surf and came to a halt. As she hadn't disrobed, he gradually moved forward to the place where terrace met dune. Perhaps she only intended to go wading? With the catlike grace of a large man who has spent a good part of his life in physical activity, he hurdled lightly over the low sea wall to the fine, cool, silky sand, only in that moment remembering that he wore no bathing suit.

What the hell, he decided with a swift downward grimace. In summertime a towel was decent enough for quick introductions between neighbors. It was not as though he intended to remove it.

The sand cushioned his footsteps as he moved swiftly forward.

But she had moved forward too, farther into the water. He came to a halt near the water's edge, realizing that she did intend to swim after all. Waves were now tugging at her thighs, wetting the edges of the T-shirt. One upward drift left ripples of thin cotton plastered over a hip, and he saw the womanly curve of bared ivory flesh beneath, enticingly paler than the golden length of her leg.

Half in the water, she balanced herself, and then she simply stood there, looking at the sea, with the offshore breeze winnowing her long hair so that it streamed toward him. The color of it reminded him of a newly peeled chestnut, warm reddish brown with a deep, natural glow.

For a moment the woman hugged her arms, suggesting that a chill had passed through her body. And no wonder, he thought. The sun hadn't been up long enough to heat the air.

Twice she raised her arms as if to dive forward, and twice she lowered them. On her left hand, which was close to him, he could see no wedding ring. Again, she stood for a moment hugging her arms. Amused, he smiled to himself and kept his silence. A neophyte swimmer? A would-be Spartan, not quite willing to take the cold morning plunge?

And then she raised one fist in a gesture of anger. Her words were low but they were fierce, and their tremble carried faintly on the breeze.

His eyebrows lifted. Had he heard right? *I'll beat you yet.* Was that what she had whispered? Or had she said anything at all? Was it only the salt breeze stirring in his ears?

He had time to wonder no more, for in a surge of silver spray, she dived cleanly into the sea and swam straight for the horizon, knifing through the water with the expertness of an excellent swimmer.

The words must have been half imagination, he decided wryly. She looked as though she had beaten that sea long ago.

He stood and watched until he could hardly see the froth of her crawl. As he watched, his appreciative smile gradually faded and a grim expression took its place. Good swimmer or no, she was going too damn far.

With relief, just as he was unhooking his towel to race out after her, he saw that she had turned in a great arc and was heading back toward the shore. He winced and stood his ground. If she wasn't in trouble, she wouldn't thank him for arriving at her side in a state of total undress. She probably wouldn't thank him for even standing on the beach when she swam in to shore; after a dunking, that T-shirt was going to be damn indecent.

With sudden decisiveness, he turned and hurdled the sea wall to return to the house, not bothering to restore the towel to his hips. From his study, he watched with narrowed eyes until she had returned to safety.

Satisfied that his help would not be needed, he turned away before she moved fully out of the water. He was a man of many faults, but voyeurism wasn't yet one of them.

But he couldn't deny that something had stirred in him—nine-tenths imagination, he was sure, for from the study door it was hard to see all that much—when she emerged from the sea with the T-shirt clinging closely. The shadow of her thighs, darkened by water, had showed faintly through the wet cloth.

And the face . . . he had seen well enough to know that it wasn't going to be a disappointment.

He went to his desk and flicked on the recording machine from which his personal secretary and Man Friday would take instructions when he arrived later in the morning.

"Top priority, Jesse. About that invitation I issued for next week. Put her off nicely, will you? For one reason or another, I think I may not want her around next week. Send flowers and compliments and something pretty, a bracelet or a gold pin or what-have-you. Nothing too earthshaking; to date she's only a casual acquaintance. And Jesse . . . soon as you've done that, find out all you can about the redhead staying in Middle Widow. And I mean everything except the vital statistics—they're perfect just as they are."

Thoughtful, he stood for a minute, not leaving his desk. Moments later he snicked the machine on again. "Strike a part of that message, Jesse. Or at least reverse it. *First* find out about the woman in Middle

Widow. If she's married, engaged, virginal, frigid, under twenty-one, currently in love or living with a man . . . or even worse if she's been showing signs of husband hunting . . . just let the first invitation stand, will you?'' He laughed softly. ''Or would you have done all that automatically, Jesse? Usually you warn me before I even ask. P.S., friend. If you arrive while I'm out this morning, I'm only off to buy a bathing suit. And to answer your other question, no, I certainly have not flipped for Middle Widow. I haven't even met the young woman yet.''

Whistling softly again, flicking his towel against his knee, he headed for the second floor. Until he got that bathing suit, a shower would have to do.

Chapter Two

*E*ven when Danielle was waist-deep again, with the safe, solid shore only a few yards ahead of her, her throat was still clutching with fear, her heart battering wildly against her ribs, her mind turning to a swirl of panic at the feel of the undertow pulling so strongly against her thighs, trying to draw her back, back, back into the sea.

After reaching solid sand, she was still quaking, breathing erratically, too enwrapped in her own internal battle to notice the footprints, far larger than hers, that ruffled the near stretch of shoreline. She snatched her towel and dashed for Middle Widow, not noticing the several newly opened shutters in the great weathered shingle home fifty yards or so to the east.

She didn't halt until she had reached the door to the study. With a key she'd left pinned to her towel while swimming, she unlocked the door and closed it swiftly behind her. Because of the valuable painting the room contained, it was climate-controlled in all seasons.

Inside, Danny leaned against the door and shook with nerves that were only gradually overcome.

"I did it," she whispered to herself as her pulse and her breathing gradually became regular enough to allow the first trickles of triumph to surface.

"I did it," she repeated aloud.

"I did it!" she shouted. She threw back her head and laughed a silvery laugh of relief. She'd braved the sea and she was back on shore!

"So *that* for old curses! So *that* for old superstitions!" She laughed again and thumbed her nose in a westerly direction. "So *that* for your stories, Emma Merriweather!"

Grinning happily in the flush of conquest, Danny vowed to herself that she would repeat the feat tomorrow. She'd do it every morning all summer long, and in time she would go even farther. If the swimming became habit, the panic was sure to lessen. And one day soon, just to demonstrate to Emma Merriweather that there was no need for quavery protestations, she'd do the swim later in the day, when the Merriweather sisters were awake and Mildred was watching with her binoculars.

Danielle twirled happily in her triumph, dripping pools of seawater over an antique Persian carpet, in a way that the tenants of the past nine summers had not been allowed to do. They'd all been forbidden the use of the tightly locked study and had had to use the side door after swimming.

A little later in the morning, she decided, she'd bike into town and buy a bathing suit to set a seal on her resolution to keep up the swimming. She needed one for sunbathing anyway. Her nine-year-old bathing suit, which she had found in a drawer the day before, had been uncomfortably tight over breast and hips. The years had rounded her curves; but then, she couldn't expect to have the same figure now that she'd had at age twenty.

Before going upstairs to shower and dress, she walked to the venerable Georgian desk and retrieved the wedding ring she had tucked onto the nose of a piece of old scrimshaw carved to represent a seal. Her smile faded a little as she pushed it back on her finger. She couldn't pretend she had fully dared the sea, when she had removed the ring with the superstitious feeling that she might be able to fool the deep into not knowing who she was. Roger had been wearing a matching ring when he drowned.

Half the trouble, Danny supposed, was that she should have gone back into the sea immediately after the accident. After all these years the going was harder than it ought to be.

As she left the study, she determinedly avoided looking at the huge, life-size portrait that dominated the one wall not covered with bookshelves, although she was aware of its haunting, time-darkened blues and greens invading the corner of one eye. Triumph was triumph, and Danny wanted to hold on to the feeling of accomplishment a little longer. If she was going to conquer superstition, she couldn't let superstition conquer *her*.

As it was early June—pre-tourist time—the boutique, which was just off Main Street in the town of

Nantucket, was empty but for the very young girl who was tending the shop. She couldn't be more than twelve or thirteen, probably a schoolgirl with her first Saturday job. She smiled shyly but didn't recognize Danielle, although several other locals had done so during her bike ride through the town's cobbled streets. Most of them had forgotten her married name, but the rich mane of Fielding hair was a trademark hard to hide.

Danny vanished into a fitting room with an armload of selections, and after a long, lingering debate with herself and her pocketbook settled on two—a sleek, skintight gold competition suit for swimming, and a delightfully indecent sea-green bikini for sunbathing. The latter was no more than several nonsensical wisps of fabric held together by chain links at the hip and at the breast. It did naughty but nice things for her figure, and the green was almost the exact color of her eyes. Danny couldn't afford it, but she couldn't resist it, either. Well, that wasn't so much, was it? Two bathing suits in nine years? Besides, she thought with amusement, it would be interesting to give starchy old Mildred Merriweather something real to be shocked about. With luck, the bikini would knock the lenses right out of her binoculars.

Finally satisfied with her choices, Danny slipped back into her white denims and navy T-shirt. The day had warmed a bit, and she hadn't needed the thin, blousy, white nylon Windbreaker she had brought along. She slung it over her shoulders as she left the fitting room.

The teenager was now looking after a tall giant of a man, but she peeked around his broad shoulders and smiled nervously at Danny. "I'll try not to be too long," she said.

The girl was partway through writing up the man's sales bill, so Danny waited, idly looking at the mound of his purchases. He'd been buying bathing suits too. At least a dozen of them. Maybe *two* dozen. My God, didn't he have any limit to his budget? With the prices in this store, his bill was going to run into hundreds of dollars.

Painstakingly, the teenager was writing out a description of each different suit—color, size, stock number. Then each bathing suit had to be removed from its hanger—a tricky task, apparently—and the hangers had to be stored in a box a few paces away. Parts of sales tickets had to be removed, and the young girl was also folding each separate purchase carefully into colored tissue paper before moving it to the other side of the counter. At times she got confused and had to retrace her steps. "Sorry, I'm not used to this," she said, worrying the end of a pencil.

"No hurry," the man said equably, in a deep, well-modulated voice. Danny turned her attention from the laden sales counter to the man himself.

As his back was turned to her, she couldn't see much except very powerful shoulders beneath a tan T-shirt, and lean athletic hips in cream-colored denims. From the lack of a label on the back pocket, as well as from the hip-hugging cut, she decided the denims were custom made. She supposed his size made it hard for him to buy off the rack. Gradually her eyes traveled upward. He was very, very tall, and although she herself was tall—nearly five ten in her flat sneakers—she had to look upward by at least six inches.

His hair fascinated her. It was well-cut where it licked his collar, but just unruly enough to leave the impression of a lion's mane. On close inspection, the dark blond was really hair of a thousand colors, tawny as treacle beneath the sun-streaked surface.

It was antique gold, she decided, finally reaching a description that satisfied her. Dark gold with polished highlights. The fuzz on his forearms, bleached by sun, was a much lighter gold—white-gold against a tan that must have been acquired under a more southerly sun. His watch was gold too—real gold, she decided, and thin as a wafer. Idly, to pass the wait, she squinted to see if it was a Patek Phillipe. She thought it was. Filthy rich, she decided, not with scorn but with mild envy, because she wouldn't mind being filthy rich for a few months herself.

By the time the sales bill was written—three closely cramped sheets and multiple carbon copies—Danny was beginning to grow restless. The young girl double-checked the amount on her adding machine and looked up with a relieved grin, her face flushed with pleasure.

"One thousand and twenty-two dollars and forty-seven cents," she said. "Mrs. Gordon isn't going to believe this. It's got to be some kind of record for a bathing suit sale." Her shy grin encompassed Danielle as well as the man at the counter. "Really, I'm sorry I took so long, but I have to confess. This is the very first time I've minded shop or made up a sales bill, and the little tags confuse me. Half the time I'm not sure which is the price and which is the stock number. Would you like to check it out for yourself?"

"I trust you completely," the golden giant said gravely. "You've been thorough and conscientious, and your employer—Mrs. Gordon, is it?—should be very, very pleased with you. Er . . . is that total before tax, or after?''

"Oh! Uh . . . before," came the flustered cry, and the young girl flew back to her adding machine.

"Five percent," the man advised her gently.

Danny hid a grin, as she was sure the man must be doing also. Now she understood why he had been watching the preparation of the bill so carefully; he didn't want the young girl to get into trouble. Nice man, she decided. Filthy rich, but *nice* filthy rich.

At last the young girl looked up again and gave a new total. The man pulled a checkbook from his left hip pocket.

"Sorry, I can't take a check. Mrs. Gordon says not if it's over fifty dollars, and even then I'd have to have lots and lots of identification."

The man restored his checkbook to its intimate niche. "That's fine," he said. "I'll charge it."

"I'll have to get authorization," the girl said, reaching for the charge machine. "May I have your charge card, sir?"

"Charge card?" The man sounded mildly surprised. "Sorry, I didn't think to bring one. You could send me the bill, though. The name is—"

The girl's face had fallen. "Mrs. Gordon says absolutely no charging without a card, except for people she knows personally."

"You can tell her I live at East Widow. Surely she knows East Widow? I thought the Three Widows were famous on Nantucket."

Danny's eyes widened. So *this* was the neighbor who had arrived during the night! He'd bought the property nearly nine years ago, subsequent to her last stay on the island. Danielle knew his name—Seth Whitlaw. She also knew a little about his occupation. His Boston-based company, Whitcraft, manufactured power boats. The Whitcraft Fisherman, now the company's foremost line, had become famous in New England's offshore waters over the past decade or so, thanks to a good, safe, seaworthy design that combined stability, streamlined good looks, and a price within reason. The new line, now being exported all over the world, had rejuvenated the venerable Whitcraft company, which had once built only expensive cabin cruisers and power yachts, rich men's toys. In New England the name Whitcraft was practically synonymous with pleasure craft; and Seth Whitlaw *was* Whitcraft.

"Pleasure boats!" Mildred had sniffed two days earlier, on Danny's arrival in Nantucket. "First time I clapped my eyes on the man, I knew he did something sinful for a living. What can you expect of someone who's been divorced?"

Mildred, who was the sensible one of the ancient maiden ladies, disapproved of the new neighbor very strongly because he'd always had female companions during his visits. "And not even the same one every time," she had added indignantly.

"But there were only three different ones in all those years, Mil," Emma had added in her anxious voice. "And on TV they keep telling us that times have changed. Isn't that so, Danny? Besides, they were all quite nice. Not at *all* like I thought loose women would be. And he's not so very bad, either. In fact, I like him. He—"

"We won't talk about him anymore, Emma," Mildred had decreed firmly. "It doesn't do to speak of the Devil in case the Devil appears. With luck maybe Mr. Whitlaw will stay away this summer, as he did most of last year." And although Emma was several years the elder, she had deferred to her strong-willed sister.

So this was the man who had bought East Widow. Well, well. Truly curious now, Danielle edged closer to the counter just as Seth Whitlaw said, "Look, if this is going to be trouble I'd better not take all those suits." Then, seeing the face of the young girl, he added, "Never mind. I'll give you cash."

Cash? Danny's eyes widened. They took in the beginnings of a strongly delineated profile—hard jaw, hard mouth, straight nose, unusual golden brows that were, unexpectedly, several shades lighter than his hair. Tiny squint lines feathered out around his eyes; small, pale bursts that had partially escaped the sun.

Seth Whitlaw pulled a roll of bills from his hip pocket and started counting them out into the girl's hand. With mild interest, Danny counted with him, staying back just far enough to escape his peripheral vision. "Oh, damn," he muttered moments later.

"I can lend you the difference," Danny said calmly, before the salesgirl had a chance to get upset. "About a hundred dollars, isn't it?"

Seth Whitlaw turned and stared as she drew the bills from her wallet and placed them on the counter, and if he had a double reason for surprise, Danielle was not to know it. His look of disbelief, a look so wide that it opened all those tiny indentations around his eyes, seemed perfectly natural under the circumstances.

The young salesgirl turned toward her cash register, looking infinitely relieved. With a frown of concentration, she started to fiddle with the keys, trying to unlock their mysteries.

Danny was smiling impishly at her new neighbor. "Really, I trust you completely," she said. "You've been thorough and conscientious, and I imagine Mrs. Gordon will be very, very pleased with you. You must have bought every men's bathing suit in the store."

He threw back his head and laughed as if he were enjoying some huge joke, and Danny felt a warm glow at the sound. She thought she agreed with Emma. She was going to like the new neighbor—and as for the woman friend he was likely to have along, so much the better. Danny thought it would be nice to have some company her own age.

While he laughed, she watched and warmed to him. She could imagine that Seth Whitlaw would appeal to women. He had good teeth, strong and even. He looked like the man of the sea that he was—rugged, loose-limbed, easy in manner, with an unpolished, larger-than-life handsomeness about him. His blond, rakehell eyebrows were just crooked enough to be truly interesting. And he had a wonderful mouth.

His eyes came back to her, and she saw that they were direct, honest brown eyes laced with amber lights that suggested a sense of humor. She held out her hand in a simple, sincere gesture. "Hello. I'm Middle Widow."

He took her hand and kept it in his large one. His fingers were warm, his clasp light but firm, and for the moment Danny forgot to draw her fingers away. "Is that why you trust a total stranger enough to lend him money?" he asked. His eyes, she noticed, were just watchful enough to tell her that he was no one's fool.

"I think I would have anyway," Danny answered, and then wondered why she felt that way. It wasn't because of his thin gold watch or his obvious wealth. A filthy-rich man who was careless with spending might also be careless with remembering about borrowed money; she knew she might never see it again. Although she could ill afford to lose a hundred dollars, at the moment she didn't care. The trust came from some other source—his consideration for the nervous young salesgirl, she supposed.

"I've heard all about you from the Merriweather sisters, Mr. Whitlaw," Danny went on. She grinned easily. "Well, almost all about you. They didn't tell me you had a bathing suit fetish."

"Maybe I'd better explain myself," Seth Whitlaw said, nodding toward the heap of his purchases. He was still holding Danielle's hand, but the contact seemed so natural that she didn't try to pull away. "I wouldn't want you to think I always buy a lifetime supply of everything when I shop. It's just that you were in the fitting room for a helluva long time, and it happens there's only one fitting room in this place. Tomorrow's Sunday; the stores will be closed; I was desperate for a bathing suit; and to top it all I don't have a clue about my waist measurement." To Danny, it looked just about right: firm, flat, and well exercised. "I usually leave details like that up to my tailor, because it's hard for a big man to buy clothes off the rack. Our young friend was being immensely helpful, but unfortunately she couldn't find a tape for me to measure myself."

And he hadn't wanted to disappoint the young girl by going elsewhere for his purchases. Danny knew that as well as if Seth Whitlaw had said it in so many words.

Belatedly, she remembered to withdraw her hand from the larger one in which it lay.

As Seth plunged on with his explanation, he half wondered why he was bothering to explain himself at all. Usually he didn't. "Actually, I only bought four different styles of bathing suit"—he chuckled—"each in four sizes. I thought I'd donate the leftovers to a boy's club or something. Sorry, it sounds crazy, but there it is. Now you know some of my worst sins. I'm impatient, impulsive, extravagant at times, eccentric at times, and damn idiotic at times—or so I'm told. Also, when I make up my mind to do something, I do it. Wild horses can't stop me."

"I would have thought that was often a virtue, not a sin," Danielle said.

The small sunbursts around his eyes crinkled into a deeper, lazier smile. "I suppose that depends on what it is I've decided to do," he murmured.

"You must be very anxious for a swim."

"I am. Very, very anxious indeed. This morning I almost raced out and took the plunge in the buff."

Danielle laughed. "Good thing you didn't. You might have given Mildred Merriweather a stroke— she's never seen a naked man in her life. Emma hasn't either, but at least she'd enjoy the new experience."

Seth lifted a brow. "And you? Would you have minded?"

Danny shrugged lightly and answered without embarrassment. "I'm not an old-fashioned maiden lady, Mr. Whitlaw. I don't shock all that easily."

"Well, that's a relief. I should hate to think you were another Mildred Merriweather, about to drop dead at the sight of a man au naturel. By the way, please call me Seth. And . . . ? I'm sorry, it seems you have the advantage of me. The Merriweather sisters may have told you a great deal about me, but I don't even know who you are.''

"Danielle Morrow. As we're going to be neighbors, you may as well call me Danny.''

He looked at her judiciously. "At the moment Danny seems to suit, but I have a feeling there are times when you're more . . . Danielle. Do you mind if I choose according to my mood?''

"Not at all.''

The salesgirl made a small sound, drawing attention to herself. Since finishing with the cash register, she had been staring at the exchange with wide eyes, but now she handed over a small amount of change. "You'd better count it,'' she cautioned.

Seth didn't bother. He stuffed it in his pocket and stood back while Danny moved forward to complete her own purchase, using a charge card. With her back turned to Seth Whitlaw, she was unaware of the lungs that drank in the faint fragrance of lily of the valley, the speculative eyes that took in the risqué little handful of bikini she had bought, the wondering frown line that slowly gathered between the golden brows, the mouth that briefly tightened into a cynical expression that was not natural to it.

Moments later they were leaving the store together. Seth slanted a sideways glance at Danny and frowned, noticing the wedding ring for the first time. When they came to a halt outside the boutique, he waved at a sleek silver Rolls-Royce parked across the cobbled street. "Transportation?''

"Thanks but no thanks. I biked into town.'' She

indicated a bicycle leaning against the shop's shingled wall. "To me, Nantucket doesn't seem like Nantucket from the inside of a car."

"But I did see a station wagon in your driveway. Your . . . husband's?"

"No, mine."

"Ah. Your husband's joining you later in the summer?"

"I'm a widow, actually. And don't bother with the condolences; I'm used to it. My husband died nine years ago."

"You don't look old enough for that."

"I'm twenty-nine."

He was looking at her with a pleasant, casually interested expression. "And in nine years you haven't corrected your single state? Don't the men in your life have eyes? There must be something drastically wrong with them."

Danny gestured dismissively. "Not them. *Me*. I haven't wanted to correct my state."

"Mmm. Too busy with your family?"

"I don't have a family."

"You're . . . not staying alone in Middle Widow, are you? It's a huge house for one person."

She smiled warmly. "As a matter of fact, I am, but I don't really mind. I'm used to the life of a loner. Although not *too* much of a loner—I'm awfully glad to see East Widow occupied. Much as I adore the Merriweather sisters—yes, Mildred too—it's good to have at least one neighbor under eighty. Will you be staying long?"

"All summer, I hope. This year my company's back-ordered enough that . . . to make a long story short, I saw no reason to go hunting for more business this year. I decided to chuck responsibility and take a long-overdue holiday.''

''A busman's holiday?'' When he quirked a questioning eyebrow, Danny added, ''I couldn't be a Nantucketer without being aware of the Whitcraft Fisherman. I hear it's steady as a rock in a rough sea.''

''Thanks,'' Seth said dryly.

''That sounds like proprietory pride. Did you design it?''

''I can't claim credit, although I like to pretend it's my baby. It sort of developed out of an idea or two I had when I was younger. In those days I was wet behind the ears, too dumb to know the ideas wouldn't work. And as I was the boss's son . . . well, the Whitcraft boat designers had to listen.'' He chuckled. ''Luckily.''

''Must have been handy, having a great big company at your disposal.''

''Um.'' It was a noncommittal answer. After a short pause Seth asked, ''You here for the summer too?''

Danny sighed. ''Yes, although mine is a working holiday, I'm sorry to say. I'll be buried in my study most of the time.''

''You're a . . . writer?''

''Nothing so simple, I'm afraid. I'm a conservator— and before you ask, that means I clean and restore art for a living. Old paintings. I've brought some of my easier commissions along to occupy the summer.''

Seth was silent for a moment, studying her with a slightly quizzical expression that suggested no overt interest. He couldn't find out *everything* in one sidewalk conversation. ''Look, it's a little late for breakfast, but as I'm fresh out of groceries in my house, I have to confess I haven't eaten a scrap today. Can I offer you a quick bite? There's a fantastic little restaurant around the corner on Main Street. When beautiful strangers come to my rescue, I always have this strong impulse to treat them to a meal.''

"Sorry," Danny said dryly, "I can't afford to lend you any more money."

"Touché," Seth said with a laugh, looking faintly embarrassed. "Actually, they know me in the restaurant. I wouldn't have trouble charging there."

"That's good, because after cleaning out your wallet, you won't be buying groceries today. Would you like to borrow some staples? I should hate to think of you starving all weekend."

Seth glanced at his watch, checking to see if the Woods Hole ferry had yet come in. "No problem. There should be food on hand when I get back to the house. Jesse—that's my personal secretary—is supposed to be coming in on the morning ferry with a carload."

Danny hid a glint of amusement. Why did he bother with the fake job description? She dropped her nylon Windbreaker and her small parcel into the carrier and reached for the handlebars of her bike. "Look, I must go. I imagine we'll connect soon."

"I imagine so," Seth agreed laconically.

Danny balanced her bike, ready to go, feeling a sudden impulse to be more neighborly, even though she had planned to spend the afternoon getting her study organized as a work space. Maybe it was simple loneliness that prompted her. The independent life—

especially when one had a solitary occupation—did have its drawbacks.

"Look, why don't you come over for an early lunch and a loll in the sun? Nothing grand. Just a loaf of bread, a jug of wine, and whatever else Omar Khayyám forgot to mention. Noon-ish, on the patio. Do you think you can stave off hunger till then?"

Seth's eyes had grown a little warier, but his answer came readily enough. "Delighted," he murmured with a faint sardonic dryness to his voice.

"Your friend too, of course. And tell her not to dress in anything more elegant than a bikini."

Her? Before Seth could say anything, Danny had hoisted her shapely hips onto the bicycle seat and pedaled off along the street.

Nonplussed, he blinked and stared, realizing that she thought Jesse was a woman. He watched with narrowed eyes until Danielle Morrow disappeared. A very, very classy woman, he decided.

And then the voice of experience whispered to him: Either that or a very clever one.

Chapter Three

From the town of Nantucket, the secluded cove of the Three Widows was only a brisk ten-minute bike ride under wind-cleaned skies, on a road that threaded past fine blue seascapes and gentle, gold-green moors where bracken grew.

Seth's Rolls-Royce passed Danielle on the road. She grinned and waved, causing her bike to wobble dangerously. He called out the window, "Forget the jug of wine! I'm bringing that." And his tires crunched away on the gravel before she could protest.

On the crest of the small hill overlooking the Three Widows, Danny stopped her bike and saw two cars in the East Widow driveway—the Rolls-Royce, plus a Chevrolet. Seth Whitlaw's woman friend had arrived, then.

She looked down at the three silvery houses with their neat picket fences, feeling the familiar glow of warmth grow in her chest. And then there was the sudden prick of tears in her eyes, the sad-sweet feeling that came from surveying a much-loved piece of her personal history. She wasn't sure why the small, poignant ache felt a little stronger than usual today. Perhaps it was because Seth Whitlaw had been asking why she hadn't remarried, and that had brought home to her the fact that there might never be direct Fielding descendants to share a past that stretched back for so many generations.

For three centuries, and until not long ago, the whole stretch of prime shoreline in the cove had belonged to Danielle's family. Because she was exceedingly proud of her heritage, on official documents she still signed her name as Danielle Fielding Morrow, although a lawyer friend had told her it wasn't strictly correct legally. Danny didn't care. She'd sooner have dropped the name Morrow.

The Fieldings, of whom Danielle was the last direct descendant, had been sea captains and shipowners with a history extending back for almost as long as the written history of Nantucket itself. The houses themselves were not as old as that. They had been constructed little more than a century before, by one Captain Jethro Fielding. Shortly after the Civil War, when several seventeenth-century buildings had burned down, put to the torch in some political wrangle, he had built Middle Widow for the young bride he had brought from France, and East and West Widow for the use of his two married sisters. The homes were large and stately and simple and all very nearly alike, with silvery weathered shingle sides, shutters, and fine widow's walks on top. Similar flat platforms graced the peaks of many old Nantucket roofs, and on those roofs, women had once watched out to sea for their husbands. The presence of a widow's walk could be detected clearly from a great distance because of the railings familiar to a Nantucketer's eye.

The roofs of the Three Widows were extremely fine examples of this indigenous island architecture and were sometimes photographed for their picturesque beauty. The particular loveliness of the land setting, the way it curved softly and melted from green-gold grass into silver sand dunes and blue sea, also invited the camera.

On detailed maps the cove was marked as Fielding's Cove, but no one ever called it that. Most people, except for locals with long memories, thought the name of Three Widows had come into being because of the trio of identical widow's walks. It hadn't. Once, there really *had* been three widows. Their story was not commonly known, but it had lingered on in Fielding memories and Fielding lore. In her childhood Danielle had heard the superstitious old tale many and many a time at Emma Merriweather's knee. She had tried to shake it out of her mind, but the story was still a part of her, bred into her bones, fed to her with her first spoonful of Pablum, and the events surrounding her husband's death made the superstition very hard to erase.

It also made it very hard for Danielle to remarry. She would have liked to marry, or at least to have a child—even one child who bore Fielding blood, even if he or she didn't bear the Fielding name.

But she couldn't, not until she had conquered her

fear of family superstition, which meant conquering her fear of the sea. That was the real reason she had returned to Nantucket. She was on the threshold of thirty, and if she didn't overcome the old superstition soon, someday all that storied property, with its dunes and its hummocks and its sea view and its beautiful silvery buildings, would belong to people who knew nothing about the Fieldings. A third of it—Seth Whitlaw's third—already did.

Instinctively, Danielle had decided she liked the newcomer. All the same, she was sorry that she hadn't somehow managed to save the property intact. East Widow had left the family with the death of her father, Captain Homer Fielding, in the tragic sequence of events that had also taken the life of Danielle's husband. The parcel of property had been sold to Seth Whitlaw at that time to settle estate debts.

But she still owned two thirds of the huge cove, she reminded herself, and two of the houses: Middle Widow and West Widow. Danielle was fiercely proud that she had saved them against all odds.

Her father's will had granted the free use of West Widow to the Merriweather sisters. The sisters were distantly connected to the Fieldings, from an impoverished branch of the family. In the way of another era, during their youth three quarters of a century before, they had been taken in and given home and shelter with the Fieldings. They had been made a part of the family. They had not even been asked to perform the genteel, ladylike duties that they had expected as poor relations, and as years went on they had devoted themselves to the family with energy and will, returning the generosity a thousandfold. Good-hearted Emma had insisted on helping with three different generations of Fielding children, Danielle included, and efficient Mildred had insisted on managing the kitchen and housekeeping staff of Middle Widow for many, many years. Now that they had retired, the west house and a pension were theirs for life, a small payment for their long loyalty.

Nowadays the risk of losing the remaining two houses wasn't great. The second and third mortgages had been paid off, and one of the first mortgages had only one more year to run. Danielle had decided it wasn't so very much of a luxury to steal one summer at Middle Widow, even though she was unhappy to lose the whopping rental it usually brought in. For the past nine years she'd managed to rent it out in winter too, although at a very low off-season rate, to a writer looking for privacy.

Writer . . . and that drew her mind back to Seth Whitlaw's wrong guess about her occupation. Mulling over the exchange in the store, she realized that he probably didn't even know she was the owner of Middle Widow. The name Morrow would mean nothing to him, as he'd bought the house from the Fielding estate. And the loyal Merriweather sisters wouldn't have gossiped about her—in fact, they'd probably had very little to do with Seth Whitlaw. Mildred, Danny gathered, had been discouraging Emma's contact with a man who to her mind was only one step short of the Devil incarnate.

Suddenly remembering that a jug of wine and a loaf of bread needed a little something to go along with them, she unbraked the pedal and allowed her bike to glide down the incline toward her house. From a window of West Widow, she saw a flutter of white handkerchief: Emma waving a greeting. Out an open door, she saw a mop being shaken: energetic Mildred keeping the house shipshape and Bristol fashion. Danny smiled because she could tell which sister was which without even seeing a face.

She waved at West Widow and went through her own front door, on the landward side of the house. The next half hour was spent in a small flurry of activity in the kitchen. With a plate of sandwiches prepared— hearty slabs of ham and cold chicken for a male appetite, more delicate watercress and cucumber con- coctions for a female one—she raced upstairs to change into her bikini.

Once in it, and about to make for the stairs again, she glanced in the mirror. She came to a dead halt. Had she really bought something *that* indecent? Good Lord, if she wore it in front of the new neighbor, his woman friend might mistake the purpose of the invitation.

Danny hunted around in her closet until she found an old thigh-length terry beach coat, a terra cotta color that didn't do much for her hair. She looked in the mirror, now satisfied. Her long bare legs were normal exposure for summer, and she'd defy anyone to say there was anything erotic about her appearance. But if Seth's woman friend did turn up in a bikini, and if she seemed to feel uncomfortably overexposed compared to her hostess . . . why, the coat could come off in a quick flip.

Danielle would have been surprised to know exactly how much Seth Whitlaw knew about her by this time. At that very moment, in the house to the east, he was being given a quick rundown by his personal Man

Friday, who in a swift, efficient phone call to a local contact—a marina owner who was the local agent for Seth's Whitcraft Fisherman—had already found out a good deal about the Fieldings and Danielle herself.

Jesse Horowitz was a short dumpling of a man in his late middle years, with a bushy black beard and a head as bare as a billiard ball. He had a passion for detail, and he delivered his information in a staccato voice, referring to notes he had made.

"I'll double-check everything," Jesse Horowitz told his employer, "but for the moment this should be relatively accurate. Danielle Morrow's husband, Roger Morrow, was a New York stockbroker, some years older than she. I don't know how she met him. Charming man, good family. Extremely wealthy family, in fact.

"He and his father-in-law—her father, Captain Fielding, that is—both died on the same day, in a sailing accident. Morrow drowned right out there"—he waved in the direction of the water—"about a quarter mile off shore. The details are a little fuzzy here, but the gist of it is this: The old man, Captain Fielding, had been handling the sailing, because young Morrow was new to the game, and also on the mend from a broken leg. It seems that Fielding had a fatal heart attack while they were at sea. Morrow tried to sail the ship back to shore, not to its regular mooring in the harbor, but into this cove, probably because it was closer and night was falling. He hallooed for help. While Danielle Fielding . . . er, Danielle Morrow . . . was swimming out, the sailboat capsized. Morrow drowned."

"That close to the shore? Couldn't he have hung on to the boat?"

"Normally, yes. He was a good swimmer and there were lifejackets aboard. But . . . his leg was in a cast at the time. He went down like a stone. Actually, Danielle Morrow was the one who spent the night clinging to the boat. She was eight months pregnant at the time. She exhausted herself diving to try and find the two men and didn't have strength to get back to shore. She did find her father and pulled him over the hull of the boat, but of course he was dead by then. There was no help for her, because no one had witnessed the accident—the old cronies in West Widow had been taking supper with some friends that evening. During the night the sailboat drifted some distance out to sea, and it wasn't found for nearly twenty-four hours. The Morrow woman lost the child, naturally."

"I see," Seth said thoughtfully, wondering if those faint words at the water's edge had been more accurately heard than he'd thought. Accurate or not, the widow Morrow had guts.

"It turned out that this fellow Morrow had been a very bad judge of the market. Greatly given to buying on margin. He'd lost his own family's fortune in misguided investments, and he had given equally bad advice to his father-in-law. When the smoke cleared, the estates, both of them, were nothing but a bunch of worthless stock certificates. At the time of the deaths, the sky had been about to tumble in anyway. Your dealer ventured a guess that young Morrow had told Fielding the bad news during the day's sail, and that that was what had caused the heart attack. And for the last little detail . . . the whole episode left Danielle Morrow in bad financial shape for a time. He doesn't know how she got out of the mess, but she did.''

Jesse Horowitz put down his notes. His mouth, almost hidden in the black beard, was somber. ''Until I find out more, don't get too involved, Seth. I haven't got a clue what she's been up to for the past few years. I don't even know where she's been living.''

Seth walked to a window from which he could see the outline of Middle Widow. He stood thoughtfully, with his hands thrust into his pants pockets. ''Thanks, Jesse. Warning noted. By the way, friend, can you lend me a hundred bucks? And cancel that other invitation, for sure.''

Barefoot, threading her fingers through her hair to push it away from her face, Danielle descended the stairs, absently feeling gratitude that the two Merriweather sisters would not be around this afternoon. They always spent Saturdays visiting some equally aging acquaintances over at Polpis. Not that Danny had anything to hide from them—entertaining neighbors wasn't exactly a sin—but Mildred would likely react as though it were. Her probing questions could be a nuisance at times.

Through an open window on the landing Danny heard the murmur of a male voice she recognized as Seth's. She started to hurry.

Like the study, the living room had doors opening onto the terrace. Although that exit was a little less convenient, especially to the kitchen, she made her way quickly toward it, carrying the tray of sandwiches she had prepared earlier. She didn't want to give Seth or his friend access to the study. She felt oddly reluctant to answer questions about the portrait on the wall, which they couldn't possibly fail to notice.

She emerged from the house with a smile of greeting that altered subtly when two men, Seth and one other, rose to their feet. There was no woman at the grouping of lounge chairs on the terrace.

Seth was in a bathing suit and T-shirt, but the bald man with the bushy black beard wore a business suit. He moved forward swiftly, surprisingly agile despite his tubbiness, and took the tray from Danny.

"Danielle Morrow, Jesse Horowitz." Seth was looking watchfully amused at Danny's attempt to hide her surprise. "You took off so quickly, I didn't have time to explain that my secretary—or to be more exact, my combination guardian angel, personal assistant, valet, general dogsbody, and Man Friday—was a male. I decided the easiest explanation was to bring Jesse along for an introduction."

"But I won't be staying for lunch, thanks all the same," Jesse Horowitz said hurriedly, depositing the sandwich tray on a patio table. "I've already eaten."

Danielle recovered swiftly. "But you will stay for a drink?" She looked around and saw that a wine cooler sat on the stone terrace near Seth's chair. "Or at least a glass of whatever you brought along?"

"I'm afraid not." Jesse's eyes skated toward his employer. "Seth's not always a hard taskmaster, but today he's left me a list of instructions as long as your arm. As they say, never put off till tomorrow what you can do today." He turned back to Danielle. "I hear you restore paintings, Mrs. Morrow. An unusual occupation, and one that happens to interest me personally. You work for some art museum or gallery, I imagine?''

"I used to, but I've recently struck out on my own."

"Is that in . . . Boston?''

"New York," she corrected, and because Jesse Horowitz was a skillful man, before he made his adieux he had found out the answers to some other questions too. He knew what part of Manhattan she lived in, the address of the studio where she did most of her work, and the names of some of the restaurants she frequented.

"Mr. Whitlaw owns a Watteau," Jesse said as he rose to his feet to go. "It's in poor condition, very dark with age. How much would you charge for doing that sort of thing?''

Danny leaned forward eagerly, unable to conceal her instant interest. Although she had apprenticed a long time to learn her profession, and had worked on some very valuable paintings during those years, since hanging out her own shingle the more challenging jobs had been elusive. A Watteau would be challenging. "I can't even begin to give you a price. I'd have to see it.''

"Good thought, Jesse. Next time you're in Boston, bring it along, will you? Might as well get it done this summer. Provided Danielle can handle it, of course."

"New clients always welcome," she said. *Very* welcome, she could have added. In her study were a number of small canvases she had been commissioned to clean, but those jobs were all very ordinary. Also, they wouldn't fill her whole summer.

Her mind started to work rapidly. A Watteau would require extremely specialized care, and it would mean bringing more equipment from New York. Her study would have to be converted to a proper studio, but she had intended to do that anyway. It wouldn't be a difficult conversion, because there was already a small washroom attached to the room, put there for her grandfather when he had been at an advanced age. A camera would be needed, and more sophisticated supplies than she'd brought with her. She'd have to see the canvas in order to judge exactly what was required. With a faint frown, she said to Jesse Horowitz, "I have a burglar alarm in my study, but please make certain the painting is adequately insured. And I hope you won't expect it done in a hurry? If it's in truly poor condition as you say, it might take weeks, even months. I couldn't touch it right away, and I certainly couldn't promise it before the end of the summer."

"I don't know if—"

"No hurry," Seth interjected smoothly. "Besides, Jesse won't be in Boston for a while. Next week I'm sending him to New York on . . . urgent business. Now run along, will you, Jesse? I'd like the rest of the answers as soon as possible." He hunkered down and uncorked the wine as soon as his Man Friday had departed. "I brought white, do you mind? It seems more summery."

"Perfect," Danielle said. Sinking back on a lounge chair, she watched him as he rose to his feet. The warmth she had felt for him earlier in the morning was a little elusive, because feelings of vague discomfort were assailing her. She realized she was too aware of his maleness. His very large size seemed far more overwhelming because so much of him was uncovered. There was a fascination to the long muscular legs with their dusting of pale hair. Her eyes crept to the very virile shapes and secrets molded by close-fitting brown and white bathing trunks, and she looked upward quickly to end the little trickle of excitement in her limbs.

And then she had to contend with the curve of his biceps beneath the gold T-shirt, the tawny lion's mane of his hair, the warm smile, and the oddly attractive eyebrows. He was a dangerously sexy man, she decided. Too dangerous for her. If he wasn't bringing a companion to Nantucket this year, she'd have to start avoiding him.

He hadn't made any overtures, but Danielle was perfectly aware of what proximity could do, especially over the course of a summer. As he handed her a glass their fingers connected briefly—a little too lingeringly, she thought. Irrelevantly, she saw that his eyelashes, though dark and heavy, were tipped with gold that gleamed in the sun, and she scolded herself for noticing.

She decided it was best to attack reality head-on. "The Merriweather sisters tell me you've always had companions during your trips to Nantucket. Wives or mistresses?"

She already knew the answer, but she wanted him to be aware that *she* was aware of his predilection for the fair sex. Also, if he had arranged a companion for the summer, she wanted to set her mind at rest. And if he hadn't . . . she thought it best to demonstrate that she wasn't wearing blinkers.

Seth looked at her almost without expression. "Mistresses," he said bluntly, then went and dropped his long frame onto a chair. He fingered his wine goblet and watched her with open curiosity. "I suppose you've been wondering if I collect women the way I collect bathing suits," he stated.

She laughed. "I confess."

"So do I," he said coolly.

That silenced Danny, and she began to be sorry that she had asked anything. She was struggling not to think of Seth Whitlaw in sexual terms, but the short exchange had caused the air to become charged with innuendo. Her green eyes had met his direct, tawny ones, and she couldn't seem to draw her gaze away. His lack of dissimulation was unnerving.

Danny wetted her lips, which had begun to feel a little dry. "When will your current companion be arriving?"

"No one's arriving," he said evenly. "Currently I don't have a mistress at all. A lack I hope to remedy at some point. I've been working too hard recently and I could use the diversion."

Danny's laugh was a little too shaky. "You're very honest, at least."

"I'm also very selective," Seth said softly. "I'm not interested in any woman who's interested in marriage. You see, I got badly stung once. I don't intend to leave myself open for another experience like that. I think it's best to lay that out right at the start."

Their eyes were still locked, the tension unbearably heightened by their consciousness of each other. Danny forced the words to travel past a lump in her throat. "With me," she said levelly, "there is no start. And I think it's best to lay that out too."

Suddenly Seth laughed easily, breaking eye contact. "This is a crazy conversation. Believe me, I'm not about to invite any woman to bed on one day's acquaintance. It's a major principle of mine to make sure first that a woman doesn't have designs of any kind." With unnerving frankness, he added, "Do you?"

Danny was taken aback; she thought she'd just given the answer to that. "Good grief, no."

Seth's smile was mildly sardonic, his eyes watchful over his wineglass. "Just checking. I've had an invitation or two in my time, but it's not every day that a beautiful woman hands me a hundred dollars and an invitation to lunch, all wrapped in one pretty package." He added with a frown, "Oh, damn. I forgot to bring the hundred dollars with me. I'll drop it over later."

Danny sipped at her wine slowly, trying to think of some way to state her position as clearly as he had. "You seem to be a little unsure of my motives," she said slowly. "Rest easy, Mr. . . . Seth, because I don't have any. I only invited you over for a sunbathe and a sandwich."

"Glad you reminded me." With a sardonic grin, Seth leaned forward on the lounger in order to peel off his T-shirt. The bronze of him gleamed in the sun, and the taut, tanned skin was smooth and hard over the ripple of sinews in his upper arms. The down on his chest was a T that diminished into a few last tantalizing, tiny golden curls below his navel. Danny tried to think of other things.

"Aren't you going to join the club?" he drawled lazily, settling back on the lounger. A bronze medallion swung against his chest. Danny recognized it as a St. Christopher's medal. Her father, a man of the sea, had worn one too. She dragged her eyes away. High on the list of men not to be attracted to was any man of the sea.

"Not at the moment. With my skin, I have to be a little more careful than you." Danny's voice was cool. "Help yourself to the sandwiches, Mr. Whitlaw. Too bad your Man Friday didn't stay. I made enough for three."

"Then I'll simply have to make up for his absence, won't I?" Seth reached for the tray, which had been positioned between their chairs. "Mmm. Watercress. My absolute favorite," he said, and after that the conversation ceased to be awkward for a time. Weather, food, and the news of the world sustained them while he demolished most of Danielle's handiwork. Seth talked a little about the sailboat he had brought to Nantucket. "As part of the holiday from Whitcraft," he noted dryly.

At last he satisfied an appetite as large as himself and settled back in his chair. "I have a confession to make," he murmured, watching Danny indolently. "This morning in the boutique, if I'd turned and looked, I'd have known you were my neighbor at once, even if you hadn't introduced yourself. I saw you on the beach very early this morning, from my window. Do you always swim at dawn?"

Danny tensed, but unnoticeably. She didn't like to think she'd been observed, even from a distance. "Not always. Do you always watch at dawn?"

Seth laughed softly. "Next time I won't. I'll come and join in the swim, if I may."

"It's a free sea." But the words were slightly icy, suggesting that she'd rather be alone.

With some considerable effort from Seth, an atmosphere of casual friendliness was soon restored. He knew how to charm women when he chose—when to set them at ease, when to throw them off balance, when to retreat, when to advance. Caution told him he'd gone as far as he wanted to for the day. At any rate, he had to know more about Danielle Morrow before he became involved.

"At first I thought you were a summer tenant in Middle Widow. I was surprised to hear that you're the owner, a Fielding before your marriage. Can you tell me a little about the history of this cove? I've been wanting to know for years. Emma Merriweather started to fill me in once, but her sister Mildred marched out looking tight-lipped and put a swift end to the conversation." He added humorously, "Protecting sister Emma from the big bad wolf, no doubt. Will you tell me about your family? From the little Emma related, I'm fascinated. The first Fieldings owned whalers, I think?"

The wine and the topic and the good listener soon loosened Danny's tongue, and she became quite animated and voluble as she unfolded some of the Fielding lore. She surprised herself by spinning yarns about one hot-blooded forebear who had reputedly killed a rival with a flensing knife, another who had sailed off to become a pirate and captured himself a bride, a third who had narrowly escaped cannibals when whaling in the South Pacific. The Fielding men had been a lusty, colorful crew, jealous in love and passionate in action. One ancestor, when his wife was being lifted into his ship in a gamming chair—a chair cut from a whale oil barrel, with ropes attached to the sides for pulling the captain's wife aboard—had instructed the deckhands to cut the ropes when she was halfway up, simply because he suspected her of infidelity. Then, according to the story, he had leaped in to save her himself. "If ye keep up the kissing, woman, then I'll have to teach ye to swim," he had reputedly told her later. "Next time I'm not jumping."

When Danny had covered two centuries, with only one more to go, she suddenly came to a halt. Her recitation of the family's history had reached Captain Jethro Fielding, and that was a tale she didn't want to tell. She stopped and wrapped her arms around herself, a slightly protective gesture.

"Not shivering, are you?" Seth asked, puzzled. The air had grown still, and it had turned into a very warm day. Besides, Danny still wore her beach coat.

"Too much sun on my legs, I think," she said, rising to her feet. "Will you forgive me if I call a halt to this? I ought to get to work, anyway. I can't think why I talked so long. Having a good audience, I suppose." It was remarkable, she thought, how much he had managed to extract from her with his knowledgeable questioning. She added, "You know a lot about the sea."

"I'm an old seadog at heart. My forebears were all seafarers of one sort or another—they started back in Salem, in the pepper trade."

"That explains it, then. Most people wouldn't have a clue if you told them the captain's wife was 'having a gam.' They'd think she *had* been playing around."

Seth chuckled, also rising. "With your male ancestors off to sea for months at a time, I suppose it did happen occasionally."

"I suppose," Danielle said, looking away and picking up the emptied sandwich tray in a gesture of finality. She gave a bright smile, not quite as natural as it usually was. "Well . . . I imagine we'll be running into each other again at some point."

"I imagine we will, especially now that we've both got the wherewithal to go swimming."

"Yes, of course," Danny said pleasantly. "Now, will you excuse me?"

She slipped through the door into the living room even before Seth had vanished from the patio. After she had deposited the tray in the kitchen, she walked more slowly to the study. Her commissions for the summer, untouched as yet, were stored along one wall of the large room, leaning against the bookshelves until such time as she had converted the space for her needs. It was not these that had brought her here. She came to a halt in front of the great portrait that dominated one wall, looking up with troubled eyes at the life-size woman it portrayed.

The subject of the portrait was striking, and so was the resemblance to Danielle. Rich auburn hair streaming in the breeze . . . a slim hand holding a richly patterned blue-green shawl that also fluttered . . . finely winged brows . . . a proud, strong, delicate chin . . . pensive eyes looking out to sea . . . a rather sad, lovely mouth that looked as though it had just been kissed by the wind.

It might have been a portrait of Danielle herself, posing on the widow's walk on a silvery, misty day, in the flowing costume of a century before. However, the sepia darkening of the varnish on the picture, a natural

result of aging, dispelled doubt. The woman in the
picture was not Danny, although she had also been a
Danielle Fielding.

A connoisseur of art, recognizing the rich textures
and colors and fine composition of the great nineteenth-
century American artist John Singer Sargent, would
have judged that the likeness had probably been painted
prior to 1874, the year in which Sargent had left
America and gone to work in Paris.

The Danielle Fielding who had posed for the portrait
had been Danny's great-great-grandmother, wife of
Captain Jethro Fielding. In the lore of the Fielding
family, it was rumored that John Singer Sargent had
come to Nantucket to paint her only because he himself
had fallen half in love with the beautiful young French-
woman who had married a rich, handsome ship's
captain twice her age. According to Fielding lore, the
young Danielle, daughter of a noble family, had run
from her native Normandy to escape family pressure
for an arranged match. Alone, at the age of seventeen,
she had taken passage on Jethro's ship to make a new
home in a strange country far across the sea, and she
had fallen in love during the voyage. There was
something faintly sad in the portrait's green eyes, as if
that foreign woman had known some pangs of home-
sickness looking across the Atlantic toward the land she
had left behind.

At the moment Danny's eyes reflected some of that
same sadness.

The trouble was, she liked Seth Whitlaw too much.
Too much. She had half-forgotten the attraction while
telling family history, but in the moment when

thoughts of Captain Jethro Fielding and that Danielle of
old had triggered memory, Danny had once again
become unutterably aware of her neighbor as a man.

And she had longed, with a strength that surprised her, to attract him. At one point she had
wanted very much to remove her beach coat. She
knew she was a shapely woman; she knew how men
usually reacted. And she had wanted to earn that reaction from him.

She closed her eyes and imagined herself naked,
with Seth Whitlaw's eyes upon her, with his hands
reaching for her, with his mouth touching her, and the
thought turned her body very heated.

Slowly, with her eyes once more on the portrait, she
removed the beach coat. She unhooked the bra top and
let it fall to the floor, and the little hooks at her hips
were unfastened too, until she stood naked in the study,
with her coverings discarded at her feet.

"There," she whispered to the other Danielle Fielding. "You see, I don't believe in the old superstition.
I'll prove it's not true. I'll prove the sea can't take me
as it took you. And it can't take my lovers either. I'll
love as you did, I'll show myself to men as you
did . . . but in my case, nothing will happen except
love. *I'm not you*. Tell me I'm not you! I survived the
sea, didn't I? I survived nine years ago, I survived this
morning, and I'll survive again. Tell me I'll survive
again!"

And then, angrily, in passion, Danny cried out loud,
"Oh, damn, damn, damn! Can't you hear me? I need
help! *I need help!*"

For a few moments she buried her face in her hands.
And then, repentant at the outburst, she uncovered her

face, already bending to pick up the beach coat. She stiffened and straightened in sudden shock. Seth Whitlaw was standing large in the doorway, looking at her with no smile on his face. His eyes were darkened, no longer gleaming with a thousand little specks of amber sun.

"Your hundred dollars," he said quietly. "I apologize for walking in, but I thought I heard you call for help. I must have been imagining things."

He placed the bills on the edge of a bookshelf near the door, then swiveled on his heel and left quickly without entering the room. It was impossible to know exactly how long he had been standing there.

But he had desired what he saw, and the desire had been a dark smoldering in his eyes, a somberness in his mouth, a tensing of the muscles about his jaw.

Slowly, once she had recovered from the shock and wrapped herself in her beach coat once more, Danny turned her eyes to the portrait again, but this time it was not the likeness that held her eyes. What she saw was the small, almost illegible legend that had been painted on the lower part of the canvas, in an obscure shadow cast by the woman's figure. The letters were so faint and blurred that they very nearly blended into the brown-gray platform of the widow's walk. John Singer Sargent had concealed them very cleverly, and one almost had to know they were there in order to find them.

> *Whoso takes this woman in love*
> *The sea shall tear asunder*
> *Untouched, untouchable let her be*
> *Or lie ten fathom under*

Chapter Four

𝒟uring the next two weeks the calendar moved into the month of July. Tourists flooded the town of Nantucket. The Three Widows, on a back road and well secluded from the mainstream, attracted none of them. Two bad squalls came and went, leaving finer weather behind. Danny converted her study for work, swam at dawn except on the two days when the weather didn't permit, cleaned a couple of uncomplicated canvases, saw the Merriweather sisters almost daily, and received several laconic invitations from Seth Whitlaw. One was to go sailing, one was to go clamming, one was to go swimming over at Surfside, and one was simply an invitation to walk fifty yards one Monday morning and have a look at an antique weathervane he'd bought for East Widow. Danny refused all invitations but the last, a five-minute exercise in neighborliness and curiosity.

She was apprehensive on the way over, especially as Seth's man Jesse Horowitz was still off in New York for his employer, on some mission that had turned out to be lengthier than expected. "He'll be back Friday," Seth mentioned when she commented on the fact that the Rolls had long been alone in his driveway. "And thank God for that. I hate cooking for myself. Jesse's not hired as a cook, but cooking happens to be his hobby. Invaluable man, that."

"What do you do when he's away? Eat out?"

"Mostly. Or mess about with a can opener. Even the best restaurants get boring after a while."

It sounded like a mild hint, but Danny didn't follow through with an invitation. At Seth's suggestion, she looked over the ground floor of East Widow, pleased to see that the home was still furnished in the old Fielding way, with many fine pieces collected from around the world by generations of seafarers. The few items Seth had added were all in keeping.

Her breathing grew markedly unsteady at one point when she was standing too close to Seth, feeling overwhelmed by his size and virile impact, remembering the day he had seen her naked. She knew he was aware of her breathing too. He gave her just one long look, accompanied by a faintly knowing smile. The silent scrutiny spoke worlds. He knew she was attracted; he knew about the dull yearning in her limbs.

But he didn't make any untoward moves during her short visit, and as she left she congratulated herself on an easy escape.

The florist's delivery arrived at her door that Friday morning. Not one box; a dozen boxes. *Big* boxes. Because of the very quantity, she didn't even have to guess at the sender. She didn't know anyone else with a penchant for buying out stores, and most of her friends couldn't afford to even if they'd wanted.

She watched in stunned incredulity as the delivery man started carrying the long fat boxes through the front door, depositing most of them on the floor because there was no more room in Danny's arms. "There's more," he said, grinning, after his second load.

"He must have bought out the entire shop," Danny muttered in disbelief.

"He did," the man said cheerily. "Well, all the fresh flowers anyway. Plants we've still got. Whoever he is, he must love you a whole lot, lady. Ayeh. A whole lot. That little box, they're right out of season. Had 'em forced somehow and flown in specially."

After the van had gone, Danny just sat down on the floor and looked at the plethora surrounding her, feeling dizzy. Finally she took a deep breath and started opening boxes, looking for the card. Long-stemmed red roses in one box. Armloads of them! Luxuriant mauve irises in another. More armloads. Then pink roses. Then white roses. Hyacinths. Yellow tulips. Tea roses. Tulips of rich, dark ruby red. Tulips the color of coral. Giant poppies. Sweet peas. More roses. Carnations. Lilies. Some of the flowers she didn't even recognize.

She found the message nestling in the smallest box of all, in a bed of lily of the valley, which was a month past its season.

"I only buy out the store when I don't know what I'm looking for. Is this it? The fragrance reminds me of you."

Danny started laughing, and the laugh had a slight edge of hysteria to it. And then the laugh stopped as suddenly as if she had been slapped, because the flowers said everything that Seth Whitlaw had not. Men didn't make this sort of gesture if their interest was idle. Sooner or later he was going to try to start an affair. Sooner—from the look of this. Perhaps she had congratulated herself too quickly.

But she couldn't deny that the unexpected, wildly extravagant gesture caused a leap of excitement, a flush of pleasure, a tingle of immense anticipation in her feminine heart.

"You might have sent some vases too, Seth Whitlaw," she groaned—a mock groan—at last rising to her feet. She couldn't think what to do with so many flowers. Should she put them in the bathtub? The laundry tubs? The kitchen sink? Even then, she imagined, there would be an overflow.

The front doorbell rang before she had time to head for the kitchen in search of containers. With the habitude of many years, Mildred Merriweather didn't wait for an answer. She opened the door and stepped briskly over a stray rose that had fallen on the threshold. Behind her, Emma peered in more cautiously, looking fluttery and excited.

Mildred was eighty-two and straight and hard as a bedboard; Emma was eighty-five and soft, crumpled by age, rather like an ancient feather pillow missing some of its stuffing. Other than that, they looked quite alike. Neither sister had been considered a beauty in her youth, but age had given them character. Each had snow-white hair, a wonderful map of wrinkles, and blue eyes. Mildred's were eagle-sharp and piercing;

Emma's were vague, hidden behind perpetually clouded spectacles.

Emma stooped down and picked up the fallen rose at the door. "Oh my, oh my," she said in awe. "Oh *my.*"

"I knew you'd be needing vases," Mildred said crisply. She had come prepared with several, neatly nested together, all of them excuses for finding out what was going on.

"They came from an admirer," Danielle said, with a helpless gesture at the flowers.

Emma fluttered. "An admirer . . . oh, goodness, Danielle . . . after what happened the last time . . ."

"Nonsense, Emma. Stop that superstitious drivel. No man can swim when he has a cast on his leg." Mildred fixed Danny with a gimlet eye. "What admirer?" She was always very direct.

"A secret one," Danny whispered, and then smiled gently so Mildred wouldn't take offense. Danielle didn't want to lie if she could avoid it, but she also valued her privacy. "It's true; he didn't sign the card."

Mildred pursed her lips. "Never you mind, young missie. You may have passed the age when I can spank a secret out of you, but sooner or later your gentleman caller will come to your door, and though I'm an old lady, I still have eyes in my head. Come along now, I'll help you put some of these to order."

"No, you won't," Danny said firmly. "I'll help *you* put some of them to order, over at your house. I was just about to bring you a few boxes, actually. What's your favorite flower, Mildred? And yours, Emma?"

Moments later the three were trailing toward West Widow, with Danny carrying three enormous boxes and the two sisters each carrying one—hollyhocks and tulips for Mildred; tea roses and baby's breath and sweet peas for Emma. Emma had also eyed the lily of the valley longingly, but she had been offered no more than a few sprigs of that.

At Mildred's insistence, Danny didn't wait to see the flowers arranged. "You've got enough of your own to do," Mildred said. "Now run along. Don't forget our supper tomorrow, six o'clock prompt."

"You won't lose your head over a few flowers, will you, Danielle?" Emma asked anxiously as Danny departed. "I'm sure he's very, *very* nice, but you know—"

Mildred cut her short. "Sugar in the water for the tulips, mind. It keeps them from drooping. And trim all the stems on a slant. That way they'll last longer. Emma, stop sniffing that rose. You'll make the petals drop."

Danny laughed softly to herself as she returned to Middle Widow. Dear Emma. Dear Mildred. Danny's mother had died shortly after her birth; Mildred and Emma together had been the mother she'd never known. With Danny's father so often at sea, they, along with her grandfather, had practically raised her. She loved them dearly.

She arranged all the flowers very, very quickly, except for the sheaves of lily of the valley. With those, she took a long time. When she finished, the whole house was overflowing with the fragrance of flowers . . . and her bedroom, filled with the delicate white sprays of a very special flower, held the loveliest fragrance of all.

There was a phone in her bedroom. Without giving

herself time to think too much, she leafed through a directory until she found the number she wanted. Her finger hesitated over the dial for no more than one second, while she reminded herself that this was easier than saying her thank-you's in person.

She recognized the voice that answered, and she was glad that it was not Seth's man, whose car she had heard driving in only minutes before. "I love them," she said, simply and sincerely, the moment her neighbor came on the phone. "I'm also overwhelmed."

Seth didn't have to be told who was calling. "Did I put the card in the right box?"

"Yes," she said. "The very right box. I'm sitting surrounded by the scent of them right now."

"Wait a minute while I get a mental image of that." He paused. She could hear him inhaling, and knew he was thinking about the perfume of the flowers. "In what part of the house?"

She hesitated. "Upstairs."

Seth laughed softly. "Thanks for the compliment. Tuck one under your pillow too, will you? By the way, how about a moonlight picnic on the beach tonight? Nothing very grand, just champagne and cheese and biscuits and a few stars."

"No thank you, Seth," she said, trying not to sound wistful.

"Not in the mood tonight? Well then, I'm glad I have Jesse to prepare for a different contingency. Just as you phoned, I was asking him if he could manage to throw together one of his fantastic little dinners for two. I believe I twisted his arm enough. Shall we say nine o'clock?"

"Seth . . ."

"I know, I know. You'd rather not risk seeing me in such private surroundings. Well, as it happens, I also have nine o'clock reservations at a pleasant little restaurant in town."

Danny laughed in astonishment. "Do you always offer this kind of choice?"

"Only when I'm trying to provide an offer that can't be refused. Come on, be impulsive. I know your birthday's not until tomorrow, but—"

"You . . . what?" Danny asked faintly.

"—I thought we'd better get an early start on it, as you're sure to be dining with the Merriweather sisters tomorrow night."

"How did you find out?"

"Easy. You told me you were born on Nantucket, so I looked up the record to see if you were telling the truth about your age."

"You didn't!"

"I most certainly did. I had to find out if you were an honest woman, didn't I? Thirty, by the way, is a wonderful year. A woman knows her own mind by then—and if she's as honest as she pretends, she doesn't keep a man waiting for answers. Say yes."

"Yes," Danny repeated numbly, as if mesmerized. And when she hung up, she wasn't sure what she had said yes to: dinner next door or dinner in town. Or maybe a champagne picnic on the beach. She supposed she would find out when Seth arrived at her door.

Danny sank back on her bed and simply looked at the lily of the valley. After a while she plucked one tiny single spray from a vase and put it under her pillow, and for a long time she thought about why she had done that, and thought about Seth Whitlaw, and thought about the Danielle Fielding of long, long ago.

"Jethro brought her to Nantucket when she was just a young slip of a thing," Emma used to say, hugging young Danny to her bosom while they looked at the portrait together. It had been in the living room in those days, in a position even more prominent than it now occupied in the study.

Emma had always related the story in a soft singsong voice, quavery even then, seldom altering a word. She herself had been told the tale back about 1912, by family retainers who had actually known the first Danielle Fielding. Because Emma was of a superstitious bent and had been at an impressionable, romantic age at the time, the tale had affected her deeply. Mildred knew the story too, but her interpretation was somewhat more matter-of-fact.

"Jethro adored her," Emma would croon. "Right after the Civil War it was, when he married her. Until then he'd been fighting with Farragut, so he hadn't had time to take himself a wife. But after the fighting he went back to plying the Atlantic, bringing immigrants to the States. He saw her being herded onto the ship with the steerage passengers and knew at once she didn't belong there. Oh, she must have been a marvel to see, tall and slim, with her pretty hair and her lovely, lovely face and her proud throat and her charming French ways. Her skin was like finest ivory, they said, and her laugh like silver, and her teeth like perfect pearls of the sea." Emma's voice would lower. "He sent his men to bring her to the captain's cabin at the start of the voyage, and some say she stayed there an improper time while Jethro tried to have his way.''

If Mildred was around, and she usually was, she would sniff at that point. "Probably did, too," she would say. "She did nothing proper in her life, that one.''

"Oh, I don't know, Mil. It's true enough that he tried to move her to a good cabin after that. But she wouldn't allow it, so who can tell what she had done with him? She said if he wanted to see her again, he'd have to come down to the steerage and visit her there. And he *did*, every day, though they didn't have a scrap of privacy, with people sleeping two and three to a bunk, and even some on the floor. Oh, she turned his head during that trip, Danny. Forced to propose on the steerage deck with half the ship listening, Jethro was. She married him at sea, but even then she wouldn't move to his cabin. She said he'd have to wait till they landed for the wedding night or move down with *her*, just to teach him what it was like to sleep in steerage, so he wouldn't ever run that kind of ship again. He never did, either. He sold that ship and bought a clipper, and started running the tea trade to China.

"Hardly a head that didn't turn when Jethro brought his bride to Nantucket. She adored him too, for he was a big, handsome, brawny man like all the Fieldings. They were so much in love, Danny, and I heard that right from the mouth of servants who'd known them both. With those looks she could have chosen her pick, they said, but she had eyes for no man but him.''

"Hmmph!" Mildred would interject.

"Well . . . all that was fine when the honeymoon was on, and the honeymoon lasted several years, while

Jethro stayed on the island and built a fine home for his bride. He hired a captain for his ship and didn't go to sea at all for a time. But then when he'd seen his new wife settled, with one child born and a second on the way, he finally went off on the clipper. Months and months he was gone, Danny, with a new daughter born while he was at sea. When Jethro came back, the trouble started. His sisters who lived to east and west were jealous, and they filled his head full of tall tales. They told him that *other* men had been looking at his young French bride. And that was because they'd often seen their own husbands' eyes travel in the wrong direction, toward Middle Widow, even back when that young Danielle had been large with child. Of course it wasn't called Middle Widow then, it was just called Middle House. The servants said she'd just toss her head and turn away, but those wives in East House and West House didn't like their men even *looking*.

"Well, I tell you for a fact, those sisters of Jethro's must have been mean, narrow-minded women—"

"Sharp-eyed, you mean," Mildred would say.

"They put the terrible idea in their brother's head. Jethro was a fine man, but, well . . . there was hot Fielding blood in him, Danny, and he was jealous. He didn't want anyone looking at his wife next time he went off in his clipper. He'd been having the portrait painted—that very portrait on the wall, yes, right there—so he could take it to sea in his cabin. It was done by *the* Mister John Singer Sargent, and if you don't know who he is, you—"

"Haven't been doing your lessons," Mildred would interrupt sharply. "John *Sinner*, they should have called him, for they say he'd been looking too."

By then Emma would be quaking with fear of her own story and would hardly hear her sister. Her arms would be hugging Danny very, very tightly. "To make a long story short, Danny, Jethro listened to his sisters. At their suggestion, he asked Mister John *Sinner* to paint that terrible, terrible message at the bottom of the portrait. When Jethro went to sea again, he left the new portrait in his wife's bedroom, where she would have to look at it every day.

"Well, those sisters weren't as clever as they thought. If you go up close and read the message, you can see it's not very clear. *Whoso takes this woman in love* . . . well, wasn't that Jethro himself? So . . ." Emma's voice would drop to a ghostly, superstitious whisper. "Of course he died at sea, Danny. A big wave got him."

"And he was only the first sinner to die," Mildred would say, pursing her lips.

"Oh," Emma would sob, rocking back and forth, "I've often thought about how that poor Danielle must have felt. Left a widow in a foreign land, with two little children, and her husband buried at sea all because of those nasty women in East and West, with their nasty ideas. A widow, so young! She had to take off the pretty dresses Jethro had bought her and put on black crepe."

"As any decent women would," from Mildred.

"For a long time she was so filled with grief and pain that she spoke to no one but her children, or so they say. But she must have been filled with a great rage, too, Danny, because she thought those women had killed her husband with their suspicions and their foolish curse. Early one night, when the worst of her

grief was over, she walked out onto the beach in front
of all the three houses, after she had put her children to
bed. She knew those men and their wives were home.
She called out so that people would look. There was a
full moon. And then she stood there and slowly, very
slowly, where everyone could see"—Emma trembled
at the very thought—"she took off all her widow's
weeds. . . ."

"Every last stitch," Mildred would insert in deep
disapproval. "Knickers too."

Emma's voice would drop to a shaky whisper.
"Well, no one knows for sure what went on behind
closed doors after that. But it was whispered that the
two husbands used to sneak over here to Middle
Widow sometimes and try to get in. And she let them
succeed, the servants said, just to get revenge for what
had happened to her husband. In time, of course, they
both died at sea. So then there were three widows."

"And that's the gospel truth, young missie," Mildred would add crisply. "So for once, pay Emma some
mind. Now look at that message and you'll see there's
hellfire waiting for anyone who carries on. Untouched,
untouchable let her be . . . and don't think Mrs. Jethro
Fielding didn't reap the wages of sin too."

"The poor, poor woman," Emma quaked sadly. "I
don't think it was *her* that was supposed to lie ten
fathom under, but whoever put that spell on wasn't
thinking very straight. She lived until her children were
nearly grown, but that was only because she didn't go
to sea for years. But then her father fell ill, and she had
to go back to France to see him. She went down, she
did indeed, on a packet somewhere in the Atlantic."

"So listen to the moral, child, for *you're* another

Danielle Fielding. Spitting image of her. Carry on with men, and the sea will get *you*."

"Even if I'm married?" Danielle had asked once at the age of twelve, when she had begun to think the tale a little farfetched.

"Of course not, if you're properly churched," Mildred had said primly.

"Oh, Danny," Emma had said, her eyes filling, "I don't know. I don't know . . . the way that curse is worded, you might be taken too. It's a terrible strong curse, for it did away with three men and one woman, too, and they all died at sea, just as it says. Even Jethro went, though *he* was properly married."

"Bosh," Mildred said sharply. "He wasn't churched when he took that young French slut to his cabin. That was *his* sin. Behave yourself till you marry, young missie, that's the moral."

"But I'm not her," Danny had said.

"You will be if you don't watch out," one sister promised grimly.

"Oh, Danny, darling, I wish you weren't her . . . but hear me out. Jethro and that pretty Danielle he married, I told you they had a daughter. We met her once when we were younger, though she'd moved off the island by then. She wouldn't even marry because she looked too much like her mother . . . *exactly* like you, exactly like the portrait. And her name was Danielle too. She died safely, with both feet on land, but that was just because she was an old maid. You *should* take a husband someday, Danny, but I just don't know—"

"Stuff and nonsense," Mildred had interjected. "She didn't marry because she was too busy cam-

paigning for the women's vote. She died with both feet
on land at the age of forty-seven, in a parachute jump
for publicity, and there was nothing very safe about
that. Served her right for being a suffragette. That's
what comes of modern notions. So take a lesson from
that, too, young missie, and remember what happens to
women who flout what's right and proper.''

In the house next door Seth Whitlaw was no longer
thinking of the scent of lily of the valley. He was sitting
morosely, listening to a lecture from Jesse Horowitz.

''I warn you, Seth, you've moved too fast. The least
you could have done was to wait until you got the
report from me. Yes, the Morrow woman is stunning.
Yes, she's spunky, going for those long swims after
what she went through. But what else do you really
know about her, beyond the fact that she lent you a
hundred dollars? No one on Nantucket knows what
she's been up to for the last nine years in New York.
And why bother asking me to investigate, if you don't
want the results?''

Seth's mouth tightened. ''I got tired of waiting,
that's all. I knew you'd be giving me the news today,
so I saw no harm in making a date for tonight.
Forewarned is forearmed. Well, go on. Is she another
Anne?''

''I don't know yet, Seth, but she could be. In fact,
there's an excellent chance that she is.''

Jesse Horowitz watched sympathetically as Seth
wiped a tired hand across his brow. After a moment of
silence he said tonelessly, ''What did you find out?''

''When she married the Morrow fellow she was
pregnant. How do you know she didn't trick him into

the marriage, not realizing he'd already squandered all his family's wealth? And here's another point, Seth. She was in deep financial trouble after those deaths—I told you that. Well, it turns out it was very, *very* deep trouble, far more than my first contact told me about.'' Jesse consulted a notebook in his hand. ''Morrow had been playing with other people's money—his clients' accounts were short. I'm not talking about a few thousands now. I'm talking about *hundreds* of thousands. Well more than a million dollars altogether, according to the detective agency I retained. Restoring old paintings, the Morrow woman doesn't make all that much. When she worked for the Metropolitan, as she did back then, her salary was laughable. And yet she paid that money off, every red cent, within a few months—before the law could start seizing her assets, namely this whole cove. So how did she do it? Yes, she sold this house to come up with some of the cash she owed. The shortfall was *still* about a million dollars. So where did she get the rest? Hmm? I ask you that.''

Seth had lifted his head and was glaring resentfully at his man. He hadn't wanted to hear news like this. ''Don't ask me, ask the IRS,'' he said glumly.

''Believe me, I would if I could. But I've checked everywhere else. There was no way for her to come up with a large sum of money like that, unless she took some man to the cleaners.''

''Maybe she won a lottery.'' Seth sounded dangerously angry now. He was speaking from between clenched teeth.

''There's more, Seth. Within weeks of her husband's death she was seen lunching very frequently with a considerably older man.'' Jesse consulted his report again. "Er . . . name of Clive Hamilton. A business associate of her husband's. The—uh, presumed liaison continued for several months and came to a halt about the same time she cleared off the debt. And to answer your next question, yes, he could have been stung for a million. He's an extremely wealthy man."

"Good god, Jesse. If she was that unscrupulous she'd be living in the lap of luxury by now. And she very clearly isn't."

"Maybe she hasn't met a rich man since. They don't grow on trees, Seth. Or maybe she's met one or two, but they weren't wearing blinkers."

"Any more little gems?"

"Not much, unless you want me to start having her friends investigated too, to see what kind of company she keeps."

"Forget it. You've already told me more than I want to hear. Is that the end of the bad news?"

"Is that the end of the sarcasm, Seth? We're talking about a lot of money, my friend. If I'm right, then the Morrow woman is not looking for small game."

"And if you're wrong . . . ?" Seth asked tightly.

"Then you'll find out in time," Jesse Horowitz said confidently. "In the meantime, steer clear. Stop doing foolish things like sending fortunes in flowers. Consider, Seth. She can't help but have a good idea of your financial status. Whitcraft is a big name now. Then there's the car, the local gossip . . . your Dun and Bradstreet rating . . . by the way, her business doesn't even *have* one . . . and as to her reputation as an art conservator, that's a big question mark too. I think you'd better not let her work on the Watteau. She hasn't been on her own long enough.''

"I can't believe any of this, Jesse. She has a respectable occupation. She works for a living. She—''

"Doesn't it occur to you that she might have chosen the occupation in order to *meet* rich men? Poor ones don't have art collections, Seth. I'm not saying I'm right and I'm not saying I'm wrong, but I am saying— be cautious. Remember Anne. Of course, the Morrow woman may not have anything quite so refined as Anne's scheme in mind. She may be a gold digger of a simpler sort—if you can call a million dollars simple. Perhaps the man felt it was worth that just to get her to bed.''

"Can it, will you, Jesse?''

Impatiently, Seth rose to his feet and went to stare out a window from which he could see Middle Widow. He was remembering something else Jesse Horowitz didn't even know about. Had Danielle's cry for help been a deliberate ruse to draw him to her study, so she could display herself? Why else would a woman strip to the skin and then cry out? He'd told her he was coming back with the hundred dollars, and maybe she'd watched for him through the window. It was an old trick of the game to awaken a man's raging hungers before trying to fleece him. Yes, very clever, he thought in a cynical frame of mind. Especially after the pretense of modesty on the terrace.

And lending that money in the store . . . wasn't that just an old confidence trick to put a man off guard? To put him under obligation? To pique his interest?

"Thanks for all the legwork in New York, Jesse. By

the way, I'll want you to head for Boston this afternoon, as soon as you've finished in the kitchen. Do you think you can have the Watteau back here by tomorrow?"

"Seth, you couldn't have heard a word I said," Jesse groaned tiredly. "Do you want another conniving female in your life? Think of what your wife did to you, Seth. Think . . ."

"Go to hell," Seth said gloomily.

Chapter Five

$\mathcal{D}$anielle, who had disbelieved the family curse during her teens and the early months of her marriage, had not yet managed to conquer all fear of the water, despite the continuation of long early-morning swims. Every rational bone in her body told her that her husband's death had been an accident, no more. But every superstitious bone—and after being raised by Emma Merriweather, and especially after the happenings of nine years before, there were a few—told her she couldn't yet risk involvement with any man. Not until she was *sure*.

Consequently, she did not choose her dress that evening for flattery, although the soft cotton and the old-rose color were indeed very flattering. The summery garment had a long row of tiny, tiny buttons up the front, the sort that practically needed a buttonhook to undo. Even if Seth Whitlaw was skillful with his hands—and she was sure he was—the very problem of working his way down the barrier of the restricted front would most certainly restore her to her senses.

The full skirt of her dress wasn't much of a barrier to anything, but she was sure he was too experienced a man to start his amorous attentions in so direct a fashion. She realized he had been very subtle— ignoring her most of the time, pretending only casual friendliness, and then overwhelming her with a sudden, dramatic flood of attention. The wait, she presumed, was so she'd have time to mull over any regrets she might feel.

Once dressed, she went to wait in the study, sitting and looking at the great time-darkened Sargent portrait to remind herself that the moment for giving herself to a man was not yet ripe. Some of her reservations had nothing to do with superstition. She liked Seth very, very much, and she thought if she was too easy—not that she *would* be anyway—he might soon lose interest in her. She didn't want that to happen. She'd had lots of approaches over the years, but no man had intrigued her as Seth Whitlaw had done. She hoped he wouldn't ask her to be his mistress, at least not in so many words. To Danielle, who valued her independence, the word "mistress" had a vaguely sordid ring, the suggestion of a kept woman, or at the very least a woman who allowed herself to be showered with furs and jewels in return for favors rendered. Having an affair had better connotations, for it suggested an emotional involvement between two caring people.

But much as she liked Seth, she wasn't ready for an

affair either. She wanted . . . she didn't know what she wanted. But she knew he would make a move tonight.

In the rearrangement of the study, it had become a workmanlike space, a repository of orderly clutter. A very large room, it had good light and ample floor space. The wide lower shelves of the bookcase had been emptied for storing canvases in different stages of restoration; as Danny had brought only small works with her, the shelves sufficed. The antique rug had been rolled and removed to bare the old pegged floor beneath. The scrimshaw collection had been put away, and the desk had been covered with a large six-by-eight of pressed fiber board, which provided a good flat working surface as well as protecting the less sizable desk beneath. Bright lights on stainless steel poles, almost like photographer's lamps, offered extra illumination. Ultraviolet light was also available when needed. A magnifying headset—an apparatus rather like Martian goggles—and a small microscope stood at the ready, because most of the work was very close, done in tiny patches, and magnification was essential.

During the past two weeks a good ventilation system had been installed, with large fans to draw off fumes from toxic solvents: that job, which had been done in a day by local workmen, was the only major renovation that had been required.

As most of Danny's current commissions were simple, her supplies were also fairly simple compared to those she kept in New York. Even so, they staggered the imagination. Clamps, sheets of special board, various mulberry papers, wads of surgical cotton, stretchers, tacking irons, and various adhesives were only a few of the things stored around the room. There were also mold retardants, waxes, surgical instruments, and putty-like compounds for patching tiny holes and tears. Neat rows of bottles filled one large shelf: the lineup included turpentine, mineral spirits, naphtha, alcohol, ethyl acetate, xylol, acetone, ethanol, and a host of other specialized fluids. Many were toxic solvents that Danny used in varying strengths, adjusting the mixture to suit the particular canvas—or more exactly, to suit the particular millimeter of canvas—on which she was working. Even simple cleaning involved far more than knowing the right solvent solution for the particular task. The solvents had to be swabbed off at exactly the right time, after they had penetrated years of grime and darkened varnish but before they reached the artist's pigments, and the split-second timing varied according to a thousand subtle clues that could be discerned only by the trained eye. Hers was an extremely specialized profession, one that took years of study to learn. Experienced as she was, Danny felt she was still learning. Every single job was a little different from the last, a new challenge to be faced.

Danny had fallen into the uncommon occupation by chance. Accelerated in her early school years, she had fitted in three years of fine arts study prior to her marriage. In the aftermath of the boating accident, she hadn't had qualifications for a job that would lead to working as a curator—her initial hope—but she had managed to secure an underpaid position at the Metropolitan Museum of Art, where she had begun to apprentice for her unusual trade. From there she had taken a job at a gallery that specialized in restorations, still assisting someone else until she learned enough to work on her own. Despite the low pay and long years of apprenticeship, she considered herself extremely fortunate: taught on the job in the school of experience, she had bypassed the need for an M.A. and, following that, a further three years of study to gain a degree in art conservation.

She had struck out independently only the year before, after deciding that she didn't want to be underpaid forever. She'd done quite well, although truly valuable paintings were generally entrusted to someone with greater expertise, a reputable conservator with years and years of experience. Those years of experience were extremely important in the field, because many tiny bits of esoteric knowledge were needed while working on old canvases. The age and composition of pigment, the idiosyncracies of a particular artist's brushstrokes, a knowledge of the artist's style and original intent—all these things were vitally important in restoration. Often, paintings had been tampered with over the years: da Vinci's *Last Supper*, for example, had been painted over by second-rate artists in crude attempts at restoration not long after Leonardo's death, when the paint had already begun to flake. To get back to his original was the task of at least a decade, still in progress.

Danny had never tackled anything half so demanding, but even to clean and repair old canvases that hadn't been tampered with took patience and knowledge. Lots and lots of it. Because of the toxicity of the chemicals involved, the work could be hazardous. It was also very hard on the eyes, which often needed to rest after a few hours of close work.

The Watteau, when it came, would be the most valuable painting she'd worked on since setting out on her own. She was looking forward to the challenge. She didn't have a whole lot of heart for the other canvases she'd brought from New York. Highland cows at pasture, done by secondary turn-of-the-century artists, were not her personal meat.

As she looked at the huge Sargent portrait, she thought to herself for the thousandth time how much she would like to be doing that task instead of the others that awaited her attention. But the Sargent would be a job of many months, and she couldn't afford the time. A canvas so valuable couldn't be hurried over.

Indeed, it was valuable, probably a good deal more valuable than Seth's Watteau. Danny knew she should have sold the Sargent after her husband's death. It would have helped solve financial problems then. But at that particular time, and with the particular lore attached to the portrait, she had had a dread of selling it, as if by doing so she would have been inviting ruin on her head. She had kept the painting, and she had used other methods to prevent financial ruin. Methods that still, in hindsight, caused her throat to go dry. Playing the stock market, after Roger's disasters in speculating, had taken as much nerve as going swimming. And using the money from the sale of East Widow as her stake had taken nerve too, because that money had been earmarked to settle other debts.

She heard the grandfather's clock in the hall strike

the hour. Before it had reached the ninth strike there was a knock at the door—the study door, only a few feet from where she sat. Nerves jumping although she had been listening for Seth for some minutes, she went close to the door and called through it.

"Come to the living room, I'll let you in there."

"Why?" he called. "Is that room reserved for disrobing?"

"Yes," she came back, and switched off the study lights before she went to admit him. She also turned on the burglar alarm, a precaution that wasn't used during the times when she needed to move freely in and out of the room.

In a putty-colored linen suit, with a cream shirt and a neatly knotted tie, Seth looked so damn attractive that she could feel her knees quiver. He walked into the living room and came to a halt, smiling imperceptibly as he took in the profusion of flowers, flowers, flowers.

"You've brought more," she whispered, feeling almost more awed by the humble bouquet in his hand than she had by the morning's excess.

It was a miniature nosegay of lily of the valley mingled with tiny, tiny dark red roses. Gravely, without a word, he raised it and started to fasten it to her dress. She felt she couldn't speak. He was so close that his breath fanned her face, and his masculine aroma, soap and spicy after-shave and the faint salty tang of the sea, penetrated even through the floral fragrances that filled the room. While he worked at the pin with a faint frown of concentration creasing his brow, she watched his face, filled with an inexpressible yearning.

His hand grazed her breast, and her breast turned to

flame. "There, that should be the finishing touch," he murmured in a warm, husky voice, at last raising his eyes to meet hers. The fingers of both his hands lingered lightly where he had placed the pin, as if reluctant to draw away. "That's so that we can carry the thought of your . . . upstairs . . . around with us all evening."

She half expected him to kiss her, and her limbs went languid at the thought. At that moment, with a dinner engagement ahead, she would not have stopped him. But he only backed away, too mature and too sure of his prowess with women to rush the intimacies.

"You must have decided on the restaurant," Danielle remarked, her eye traveling over his superbly tailored clothes. She smiled guardedly, striving to overcome the temporary weakness engendered by the romantic, old-fashioned gesture of the nosegay. "Dare I ask if I'm right?"

Seth's confident smile, and the slight amusement creasing the edges of his amber-flecked eyes, promised that all secrets had not yet been revealed. "No, you may not. If I told all, it would destroy the element of surprise."

Although he had arrived at the back of the house, he led her out the front. His car was in his own driveway, and it was toward this that he guided her. It would indeed be the restaurant, then, Danny decided. She was glad of the darkness, which would prevent the Merriweather sisters from knowing of her date. Emma would be in a panic because of her superstitious nature, and Mildred would disapprove on general principles, simply because the escort was Seth Whitlaw.

It was a fine night, and after they were on the road to town, Danny depressed the button that sent the car window down in a slow, controlled flow of perfect engineering.

"If you do that," Seth remarked, "you won't be able to balance a dime."

"Balance a dime?"

"Yes, on its side, while the car is traveling. I don't believe a word of it, but that's what somebody used to claim. Actually, I don't know if it was Rolls-Royce—it might have been Chrysler or Cadillac or Lincoln or some other car maker altogether. Never mind; it could have been Rolls. But perhaps you aren't interested in balancing dimes?"

Danny laughed. "It sounds like a lot more fun than balancing dollars."

Seth was silent for a moment. "I imagine that's a trick you're very good at too. You can't earn much restoring paintings."

Danny sighed. "I admit, it's not one of your basic top-dollar professions. In fact, when I was apprenticing it used to seem like one of your basic bottom-dollar ones. But I stumbled into it, and at the moment it's the only expertise I've got."

After another small silence Seth asked soberly, "With an occupation like that, how on earth can you afford to keep Middle Widow going? And don't you own West Widow too? They must cost a fortune to keep up."

"Do we have to spend the evening talking about my finances? I'd rather balance dimes." She fished in her small evening bag to find one. For a moment she tried it on the dashboard, but it fell in the rush of air through the window, and she gave up without chagrin. She combed her free-flowing hair with her fingers, knowing joy in the race of the wind. She felt years younger, almost back to her carefree teens.

"Would you believe, this is the very first time I've ridden in a Rolls? I think I could get used to it."

"In that case," Seth said dryly, "you'd better change professions."

She shot him a small glance, mildly troubled by something in his voice. "I don't want to, actually. I've always been interested in art. And restoring has its fascinating moments."

"Such as?"

"Sometimes a conservator uncovers details that have been hidden for years. And once, when I cleaned an old canvas for someone, I found some clues that made me wonder if the painting wasn't more valuable than had been believed. It turned out to be a minor master, worth thirty thousand dollars."

"Must have been a nice windfall for you."

"For me? Good heavens, no. For the owner. But I did get a wonderful dinner out of it, in gratitude." Danny laughed. "And then the owner sold the painting and left the country without paying my bill. I was pretty naive at the time—I had made the mistake of releasing the canvas before collecting."

"That's a helluva note!" Seth's brief grin faded into a more unrevealing expression. Idly he asked, "I suppose he was a rich man too? You must meet some in your work."

"Unfortunately, no. The really rich clients don't

come to me yet. I have to build up a reputation first. In a year or two, though, I expect they'll start.''

''Is that why you went on your own?''

''Of course,'' she said promptly. She added after a hesitation, ''Frankly, your Watteau will be the biggest thing I've tackled since setting up shop on my own. I shouldn't tell you that, because you may decide not to entrust it to me. Before you renege, though, I'll also tell you that I've done paintings equally valuable in the past. I'm very good, really.''

''I won't renege. Jesse's a very cautious, very thorough man, Danielle. Keeps me from making impulsive mistakes. Naturally, he's been checking out your qualifications.''

''Oh.'' For some reason, that made her feel vaguely uncomfortable. ''And did I pass?''

''The Watteau's going to be delivered into your keeping tomorrow. Does that answer your question?''

''I'm glad you trust me,'' Danny said softly. And found that she was glad. *Truly* glad.

Seth's grim smile of acknowledgment soon faded. ''Perhaps you'll be disappointed when you see it. It's a dingy thing.''

''It won't be when I'm finished,'' Danny said confidently. ''It sounds as though you're not at all fond of the painting. I take it you didn't buy it yourself?''

''No; it's been in my family for years, acquired along with a bunch of other miscellany by some nineteenth-century ancestor who was an art fancier. I won't call him a collector, because I don't like his taste. As far as I'm concerned, the best thing about the Watteau is its frame.''

Seth slowed to enter the town of Nantucket and remarked in a casual drawl, "Must have been a big disappointment not to have a small share in that big find you made. In all these years, haven't there been any lucky windfalls for yourself?"

"Sure. Last year I won ten jars of homemade quince jelly in a raffle." Danny's voice was dry. "I've still got nine of them. Do you happen to be a quince jelly fan?"

Seth felt amusement tugging at him, despite a personal vow not to allow Danielle Fielding to enchant him in any way, beyond the obvious one in which she'd already succeeded. "Perhaps we can make a joint donation to some charity. Your quince jelly and my bathing suits," he chuckled.

"You bought all those suits just to give that young shopgirl a boost in morale, didn't you?"

"We . . . ell. I have to admit that had some bearing. She got very nervous when she couldn't find a tape measure. And then she tore a bathing suit trying to take it off the hanger, and she practically cried. She thought her employer was going to be angry with her. She wouldn't let me buy the torn bathing suit, so . . ."

I love you for that, Seth Whitlaw, Danny thought to herself. She turned in her seat so that she could have the pleasure of watching him—his big, gentle, capable hands reflected in the light of the dashboard, his shadowy face with the eyebrows faintly lit above the dark pools of his eyes, his large, handsomely proportioned body with the legs almost too long for comfort in the confines of a car. Warmth grew slowly in her chest, until the swelling sensation seemed to fill her whole being with a great, dizzy, glorious glow.

No, it can't be, she thought, her smile gradually fading. I can't be in love. Not *really* in love. Not with a man I've known for only a few weeks. Not now. Not yet. Not when I haven't conquered all the old taboos that lie in my own mind.

I cannot be in love with Seth Whitlaw.

But she knew she was.

To Danielle, it was such an overwhelming, earth-shaking discovery that she didn't even notice he had driven right through town and emerged at the other side, his headlights lancing the darkness that enveloped the island. She was looking at the faint glow of his face in the reflection of the dashboard, with the discovery of her feelings thundering through her head and her heart.

The vertigo of the moment and the blanket of the dark night seemed to swallow her into a time warp, so that later she wasn't sure how long she had sat there staring and yearning, in a haze of wonderment and sweet surprise, listening to Seth's occasional wry remarks, loving him, absorbing him through her pores.

At last Seth brought the car to a halt, and it wasn't until he left the driver's seat that she considered her surroundings. She looked around, half dazed, and realized that they were no longer in the town. She wasn't sure where they were, because she had no idea which turns Seth had taken or how long she had been watching him. The Rolls had been pulled off the road onto a dune, and beyond lay the bone-white gleam of moon on sand. At water's edge, the beach was lapped by the quiet, untroubled ripples of the Sound.

Danielle shivered, not with chill, but with expectancy and consternation. She huddled her hands around

her arms and felt the crash of her heart against her ribs.
In a place as private as this, anything could happen.
She wanted, longed, feared . . .

Untouched, untouchable let her be

The message was subliminal, and although the
unsuperstitious Danielle rejected it, a primitive part of
her knew it was there.

Seth was already opening the Rolls door for her. She
stepped out, reverberating to the light guidance of his
hand beneath her elbow. Her breath caught in her
throat. Their very aloneness was a confirmation of his
intention. She thought she ought to refuse to stay . . .
to insist that he take her home. But at the moment, with
discovery trembling through her blood, she was incapable of insistence. She wanted to be exactly where she
was, close to Seth on a moonlit beach, touching him,
discovering him, reacting to the maleness of him,
warming to the heat and the height of him, feeling the
awe of being wonderfully, deliriously in love with a
man she could admire. She felt as if she had loved him
always.

As her high heels sank into the sand, Seth steadied
her. She melted against him for a moment, feeling
dizzied by his nearness.

"You're shivering," he muttered, moving his hands
over her skin. The slow way he smoothed her upper
arms was a caress that only increased the quiver. What
she wanted, he wanted too, and the wanting was there
in the gentle, wooing movements of his fingers.

"I'm not . . . cold," she jerked out, pulling away a
little.

Seth chuckled huskily. "Is there some other cause, then?" he asked, and his voice was like the slow sea waves lapping on the near night shore.

"No, I . . . it's the surprise. I thought you were taking me to . . . to a restaurant in town." The car door was still open, its light spilling into the night. She was mesmerized by its glint on his cheekbones, by the hard, sensuous line of his mouth, by the caverns of shadow that half concealed his eyes. Seth reached up and touched her hair lightly, running his fingers alongside her temple until they hovered enticingly near her ear. The touch was the barest of brushes, moth's-wing soft, unspeakably erotic, and his breath was so close it mingled with hers.

She moistened her lips and allowed them to part slightly for the kiss she thought was coming. Her eyelids were laden with longing.

Seth allowed the expectation until the pull of sexual attraction began to cost him his own control, and then he eased away, reminding himself that he ought to explore the consequences before exploring the woman. He'd be able to judge soon enough. If she pretended to hold off, after the strong signals she'd been sending, then she was simply holding out. And he had no intention of allowing himself to be excited into vulnerability. Once in the heat of passion and past the point of control, he might make promises he didn't want to deliver. If anyone was to lose control tonight, he intended it to be her.

Alone on her own two feet, Danny tried to pull herself together. Seth was affecting her too much, and she had to maintain some distance. The taboos of the past were powerful ones indeed, and she reminded herself with a touch of desperation that she'd have to think out the situation later, in private, when Seth wasn't around. She couldn't allow him to become her lover, not tonight.

"I can't think why I shivered," she said, not wanting him to detect the extent of her weakness for him. "Really, I'm quite warm."

Seth started to remove his suit jacket. "All the same, it would never do for me to have a cold woman on my hands, would it?"

The cool observation was equivocal, and Danny felt slightly unsettled by it. No doubt about it: she was in a weakened condition. She stood compliantly as Seth draped his jacket over her shoulders. The virile body heat of him enveloped her in a new attack on her senses. For a moment she closed her eyes and swayed, but recovery came swiftly. She realized Seth was looking at her almost curiously, certainly with a watchfulness that was not quite that of desire. She began to wonder if his intentions were all in her own mind.

"Those shoes are going to cause trouble," he noted, looking down at her feet. "They'll have to come off."

That could be the first step on a journey to more removals. "I'll manage," Danny insisted.

"Sit down," Seth ordered sternly, and his hand guided her back into the seat of the car.

Without ado, he kneeled and started to remove the shoes slowly, with a hand clasped lightly around each silk-sheathed ankle to steady it while he eased the straps from her heels. It was a simple enough gesture, but to Danielle in her vulnerable frame of mind, there seemed an extraordinary intimacy to it. She could feel Seth's warm breath strike her knee.

As he finished, his fingers trailed lightly against her leg. In a swift movement he bent forward and pressed his parted lips against a calf. His mouth moved upward in a swift, moist trail, but halted at the knee when a soft involuntary gasp left her lips.

He glanced upward with mockery gleaming in his eyes, his expression clearly illuminated by the car's roof light. Danny's eyes were closed tight and she was biting her lip until it hurt. The damp imprint of his mouth felt like a brand mark.

"Your nylons should come off too," he noted. He didn't remove his hand.

Danny shot to her feet, spirit restored. "If I decide on baring my legs tonight, Mr. Whitlaw—or any other part of me—I can do it quite well on my own. Do you want some help carrying the picnic things? I'm starved."

Seth rose also, his powerful body lithe as a giant jungle cat's. Danny saw that his eyes had turned faintly cynical and guarded, and the derisive little smile that tugged at his lips held a knowing twist that troubled her. She realized he was perfectly aware of her physical reactions, and probably guessed about all the little quiverings he aroused so easily, with such light, sure, tantalizing touches.

"I'm starved too, Madame Morrow. I can hardly wait to satisfy my appetites." His voice was so casual that she wasn't sure whether his innuendo was deliberate or not. "Which would you rather carry, the food . . . or the blankets?"

"The blankets," Danny said coolly, in case he had thought to unsettle her with their mention. She had the feeling that he was playing games with her, trying to unbalance her while remaining slightly detached himself.

With suit jacket off, Seth's silky shirt molded his muscular shoulders, and Danny watched with great inner perturbance while he opened the back of the car and started handing out things she hadn't noticed earlier. She was given a flashlight, unneeded because of the moon's brilliance, and an armload of car rugs and mohairs. Seth himself took charge of a large picnic hamper and an oversize beach bag.

The beach bag was explained after they trailed toward a spot Seth picked, past the high hummocks of the dunes and onto a smooth stretch of dry, fine, silvery sand. He waited while Danny spread a blanket, then dropped his own load at its edge. "I brought beach towels too," he explained with a sardonic grin, "for both of us."

Danny's smile became a little too fixed. It was not thoughts of swimming naked that flashed into her mind, but thoughts of swimming by night. Subliminal flashes came to her: the blackness of the sea, the slipperiness of the capsized hull beneath her numb arms, the vast exhaustion, the struggle not to let go. . . .

The sea shall tear asunder

She shifted restlessly on the blanket and adjusted her full skirt to spread it in a protective tent over her knees. Her nylons were still damp where the flicking fire of

Seth's tongue had passed, breeze-chilled now to remind her of the erotic gesture. The pit of her stomach quivered expectantly because she knew he would want to kiss her more thoroughly before this night was through.

The pop of a champagne cork broke the spell of her own thoughts, and moments later Seth handed her a glass.

Danny sipped, feeling the tickle of bubbles in her nose dispel her more difficult musings. "I would have dressed quite differently, if I'd been able to outguess you. Jeans and an old T-shirt would have been much smarter."

"It wasn't me you had to outguess, it was the weatherman. I wanted to be sure we'd have a fine, clear, warm night for this. I didn't make up my own mind until half an hour ago, when I picked you up. Until then, I'd been edging toward the idea of a restaurant."

She slanted a glance at him. "What made you change your mind?"

"Those tiny buttons on your dress," he said softly, with his eyes lazing over her curves. "They're a definite challenge to a man's ingenuity."

"Seth, I—"

"I remember, Danielle," he said mockingly. "You prefer to bare things on your own, in your own good time. Now relax, pretty lady. For the moment, I'm too damn hungry to be making passes. What can I start you with? Smoked salmon? Pâté?"

As they ate the delicious provisions, Seth admitted that the contents of the hamper, and not an intimate dinner for two, were the result of Jesse's efforts in the kitchen of East Widow. Danny found herself laughing, talking, relaxing . . . and growing soft and syrupy inside every time she looked over to see Seth's easy length sprawled beside her. He had shed his tie and loosened his collar. The cream fabric of his shirt seemed to absorb moonglow, leaving the hollow between his collarbones dark and mysterious. She wanted desperately to touch it. By night, his eyes were dark and mysterious too.

Danielle was still in a glow of wonder about the feelings inside her, and they ran like a silver thread beneath the easy, inconsequential chatter of the picnic. Seth's small advances and retreats hadn't really alarmed her; they had fed her longings. Several times, she found herself touching her leg surreptitiously where his mouth had touched, wanting to feel that intimate flame again.

But she knew she could encourage nothing. And she knew she had to state her position, before Seth made his move.

At last the provisions were packed away, and silence fell. Seth lolled against the blanket, his long legs extending over its edge. Danny sat huddling her knees and looking around the site. "Nice beach," she observed casually. "But we could have picnicked just as well at Three Widows."

"With visibility like this? And Mildred Merriweather in the offing to watch? No thanks."

Danielle manufactured a light laugh. "Good heavens, Seth. It's not as though we're teenagers, about to start necking under the stars."

Seth shot her a look, and she turned to face him

directly, with a calmness that was surface-deep. "I wanted to make that clear at the start," she said. "I don't believe in leading a man on, if I'm not prepared to put out. And at the moment, I'm not."

"If you're not, then you have nothing to worry about," Seth said casually. "I never force unwilling women. It's against my principles to take advantage of the weaker sex."

"It would be easier for all concerned if you didn't start anything."

"Because you're not prepared to finish?"

"Exactly." She allowed that to sink in. "As long as you understand."

That brought only silence from Seth, and made Danielle overly aware of the vastness and emptiness of the romantic, star-strewn night. She felt utterly happy in her love, and unutterably sad because she couldn't do anything about it. She turned away from him and rested her chin on her knees. The great sea lay before her, shining beneath the moon, reminder that she had not yet laid her ridiculous fears to rest.

At last Seth spoke. "Is that a polite way of telling me it takes more than flowers in your case?"

"I wouldn't have put it that way, but . . . yes."

His hand drifted sideways and connected with the curve of her hip.

Her hip burned. For a slow time, his fingers moved erotically, defining her shape with the lightest of feathery touches. She felt she must move or scream or respond, but could do none of these. She sat rigidly, breath bottled, her entire being centered in the inches where his languid fingers roved.

"I want to kiss you, Danielle Morrow," he murmured at length, "but it's hard for a mature man to kiss a beautiful woman without wanting more."

"Then you'd better not kiss," she whispered, and her heart was large in her chest, hurting, hammering.

Seth came to a sitting position behind her, and his mouth sank into her hair. His hands moved around her, and his fingers brushed fleetingly across her bosom. Detecting the tautness of her nipples, he cupped her breasts lightly, so very lightly that she could feel no more than a grazing touch that enflamed, but satisfied nothing. "I'll proceed at my own risk, then," he murmured. "All you have to do is say . . . no."

She raised her hands to stop him, but her fingers misbehaved. With a shudder of willingness, she clasped his fingers hard against her and laid her head back against his shoulder, moaning.

His breath started to grow ragged. "You want me too. Tell me you want me."

"I don't," she groaned. "I—"

But she did nothing to stop him when he eased her slowly backward, supporting her with an arm. Danielle found herself lying prone, with his powerful arms pinioning her lightly to the blanket. Now that he was in the dominant position, his mouth made small ardent forays against her throat and her jaw, and the moist trail almost destroyed her will.

"Tell me to go on," he whispered, and his words were an erotic temptation stirring against her ear. He stroked her hair away with the extreme gentleness often exerted by large men confident in their strength and unwilling to misuse it. "I want to make love to you,

Danielle. To see you naked . . . to see you in the moon . . . to kiss you, every beautiful part of you . . . I want to make you tremble to my touch . . . to hear you cry for me to enter and take what I want . . . and give what you want . . .''

She moaned and whispered his name; and if she tried at first to twist away, she also denied the fact of her resistance by lacing her fingers forcefully into his hair.

His mouth moved onto hers. His kiss began slowly, but the stab of his tongue was sensuous and insistent. He demanded response, and because she loved and wanted too, she gave it. Her lips parted, surrendering helplessly to her own hunger and to his mastery. Her arms crept around him. She felt the body heat beneath his thin shirt, the powerful intensity in his broad, muscular shoulders, the weight of his chest against her breasts. In the weakness of her own wanting, she abandoned herself to the wonder of the kiss that invaded her and commanded her so easily, so deeply. His teeth nibbled, his lips moved provocatively, his tongue probed and dipped and sipped with leisurely expertise. He drank from her mouth until it seemed that the mingling tastes and textures had become one.

At last he lifted his head and raised himself on an elbow until he hovered over her. ''Consent?'' he asked huskily.

In the same moment she realized that his powerful hand had come to rest at the waistband of her nylons. His fingers, insinuated lightly at the edge of the undergarment, had connected with bare flesh. Her heart palpitated wildly as she became aware that during the impassioned embrace, Seth must have pulled the skirt of her dress upward. It lay tangled about her waist. By moonlight, she saw the long, smooth line of her legs revealed by the disorder of her clothes. She had forgotten herself in the kiss.

And Seth was well and truly aroused. He lay sprawled half over her, and the powerful confined contours of him throbbed against her hip.

"Consent?" he repeated more fiercely, but he moved away from her a little, so that the swollen surge of his body no longer rested in such close tandem.

Danielle's thighs were honeyed with desire. If any word had come to her lips, it would have been yes, and she couldn't say that. Nor could she voice a no, and so her throat was blocked. With her eyes bonded to his, she shook her head, her jaw locking with the effort of preventing her own verbal acquiescence.

"Say yes or say no," he ordered even more harshly, "but say it plainly. I don't like mixed messages."

Still, she couldn't answer.

Seth moved his fingers upward, to the topmost of her tiny buttons. He was more in control now, his jaw tight with the effort, and something hard had entered his eyes. He flicked one tiny button loop open. "Say no and I'll stop," he said, his voice forced, as if under pressure to find its way past his teeth.

Danny lay in frozen silence, eyes locked to his, body locked in a desperate tug-of-war between desire and will. She felt a second button go. And a third . . .

By now, the burning and freezing that consumed Danielle, binding her in statue stillness, resulted in part from the scorn that was growing slowly in the shadowed eyes impaling her. It chilled her that Seth should look at her in such a way. She didn't understand the depth of his contempt, and yet with one small corner of her mind she knew she deserved it for allowing him to continue.

Seth's fingers inched downward even more slowly than was needed. "I'll stop exactly when you tell me to in words, and no sooner," he warned with velvet softness, and she felt his fingers intruding near the hollow between her breasts. Longing consumed her, a furnace of flames licking downward in advance of his touch. With deliberate slowness, he detoured to the brassiere clip. His fingers rested there as he watched her mouth, waiting to see if she would object.

When she did not, he flicked the clasp open contemptuously, not yet bothering to take advantage of what he bared. He continued the tormenting journey to her waist, where he unfastened the narrow belt and the last of the hooks that confined her clothing.

Unhurriedly, unstopped by Danielle, he eased the front of her dress apart and pushed it to her shoulders. He didn't take his eyes from her face. She felt his fingers brush over the budded nipples to test their tautness, and she saw his mouth curl with outright contempt as she went tremblingly rigid, fighting the exquisite torment of his touch.

She started to shudder all over, choking back the "yes" that wanted to be said, trying to force an unwilling "no" through stiff lips that felt incapable of the word.

At last Seth looked downward to see the pale, moonlit curves submitting to his fingers, and the freeing of her eyes also freed Danielle from the chains of sexual torment. She gasped and twisted away, sobbing out the word that had eluded her for too long. "No, no, *no* . . ."

Seth rolled away at once, accepting the rejection with remarkable equanimity. He sat and watched with heavily hooded eyes, his mouth impassive, while Danielle also jerked to a sitting position, clasping her loosened clothes against her breasts. Breathing heavily, she started to choke out an apology.

"You can forget that part of the act," he drawled.

"Act?" She stared at him, and her throat started to hurt. Her brain felt numb, and the numbness traveled down to the fingers clutching her clothes.

Seth's voice dripped cynicism. "You've established the really important things, haven't you? You're a wildly passionate, incredibly beautiful woman who can hardly wait to lose herself in my arms. Naturally, along with your refusal, you've managed to let me know exactly what I'm missing out on. By this time, according to plan, I guess I ought to be filled with an insatiable thirst for the conquest of Danielle Morrow."

"Seth, I—"

"Am I now supposed to start offering gifts more permanent than flowers? Well, frankly, Danielle Morrow, at one time or another in my life, I have been generous with women who please me. Did you guess that? Is that why you asked about my mistresses? Were you hoping to find out if they were paid—and if so, how much?"

He seemed like a stranger. His mouth had grown stern; his jaw was like rock, his voice embittered.

"Well, Danielle, you don't know me very well. I

have taken a few mistresses, and I have treated them well, but I prefer to be pleased first . . . not teased! If you'd stated your terms bluntly, I might have listened. That at least would have been aboveboard. Or are your terms going to be a little too rich . . . even for *my* bank balance? Is that why you haven't stated them? You're a very clever lady, Madame Morrow, but you'd have done far better with me if you'd been straight. As far as I'm concerned, women like you are poison. So forget any schemes you may have in mind." His voice was low, slow, and lethally quiet. "After tonight's performance, you are not going to get one . . . red . . . cent out of me."

Danny was rigid with disbelief. He might as well have called her an expensive whore, or worse. She could not believe he had been harboring such a horrible opinion of her in his head, while all the time she had been drinking him in, admiring him more and more with each passing minute, allowing herself to fall hopelessly, head-over-heels in love. And thinking that maybe he was falling a little in love too. That was the worst of it: loving him.

She felt unclean, sullied, soiled, angry, helpless, hurt.

It was a feeling so powerful, so immediate, that her next move was not cognitive. She flashed to her feet and ran for the water, choking, shrugging off her dress as she went. She had to clean away the foulness.

Sobbing, she splashed through the shallows and sliced into the dark water. Her loosened brassiere constricted her arms, and she tore it off and hardly knew what she had done. It swirled away into the sea.

She raced for the horizon, feeling the filth of his innuendo gradually wash away with exertion and the flow of black-satin water over her skin.

She finally slowed, too exhausted to go farther, and treaded water while she became aware of where she was and who she was and why she shouldn't be here, so far from shore in a night-black ocean, with only a mysterious moon to guide her back to land.

The sea shall tear asunder

A faint scarf of cloud trailed across the one white beacon in the darkened world, and panic started to swell inside her, a living thing that could become larger than she if she allowed it to. There had been no moon on that other night.

She heard Seth's call, and turned in the water, and saw the faint phosphorescent trail left by the splash of his limbs. He was following her, but at some distance, for he had had to pause to shed his shoes and clothes. She kept her eyes on the phosphorescence and fought the hydra of panic rearing inside her. The moon was again full and clear. She forced herself to start breathing evenly, regulating the breaths by counting as she inhaled and exhaled. Seth lifted his head to shout to her occasionally. The sound of another person calmed her a little more, called to the voice of reason in her own head. *Hold on, Danielle. Hold on. You're going to survive.*

In her state of tiredness, she knew she must swim slowly or risk cramps. Quietly, quelling the destructive instinct to hurry, she started an extremely slow, measured breaststroke toward the shore.

Seth saw her coming. He swam quickly to reach her; then, without another word, he turned in the water and started to swim beside her, pacing his movements to hers.

Her seminudity didn't seem to matter to Danielle when she reached shore. Nor did Seth's nakedness— she was hardly aware of it. The sand was good and solid beneath her feet and seemed more important than the air that chilled her soaked skin, causing uncontrollable shivers. Quietly, with unconscious dignity, she slipped out of her soaked nylons and briefs and left them lying near the water. She walked away from them as if they didn't exist.

Seth was moving beside her. He said something— she didn't know what. She didn't answer him. Her face was very pale, very set. She felt completely calm now. Not looking at Seth, she aimed for the picnic site. She walked past her discarded dress without even looking at it, but Seth stopped and stooped to pick it up.

After Seth had come to a dead halt, he simply stood and stared at her water-slicked body retreating toward the blanket. He could see long trickles of water streaming from her hair, down her slim, proud spine, and he felt mesmerized, caught in a mesh of moonlight, unable to move even to clothe his own nakedness.

Danielle, numbed by some natural protective novocaine, reacted with no self-consciousness. At the moment dignity seemed far more important than nudity, and she moved with her head high, her shoulders erect. She was only distantly aware of Seth, and the awareness was confined to knowing that she couldn't, wouldn't show any sign of weakness in front of him.

As Seth watched in silence, naked on the beach,

there was a huge turmoil of emotions in his chest, the largest of them a helplessness so vast it left him feeling drained. He watched her fish a large towel from the beach bag, watched her serenely dry her body and then her hair. He saw everything, stored everything, lusted for everything—the moonglow of her nakedness, the ivory milkiness of her breasts, the perfect curve of her hips and the haunting, shadowed triangle of her thighs.

If she had set out to defeat him, she was most certainly doing it.

Chapter Six

*D*anny's internal anaesthetic had largely worn off by morning, and she recognized the cold, diamond-hard, determined feeling that had slowly taken its place. It was pride. Good, old-fashioned chin-up pride strongly laced with righteous anger. She would have liked to tell Seth what she thought of him, had it not been for one overriding factor. She didn't want to see him again. She made up her mind that she was going to fall out of love as swiftly as she'd fallen in, if she had to cut her heart out piece by piece to do it.

At dawn, on waking, she went and closed every single shutter on the east side of the house, simply so she wouldn't have to see any more of him than necessary.

And then she made the rounds and opened them all again, simply so he wouldn't know she gave a damn whether she saw him or not.

During her early morning swim she was too boiling mad to remember that she was frightened. She wore her tiny bikini and hoped Seth's bad conscience had awakened him early, so he could take a good look. Let him eat his heart out.

After breakfast she spent an hour stuffing fresh-cut flowers into huge green garbage bags. She'd done the lily of the valley the night before and flung the windows wide to air her bedroom—and even then she hadn't slept in that room because the fragrance still lingered. She'd opened a musty guest room and fallen like a log onto an unmade bed. Still numb at that time, soporific in the wake of her trying night swim, she had slept dreamlessly.

This morning, for good measure, she opened the green plastic bag containing the lily of the valley and dumped the contents of the kitchen catch-all on it. Old potato peelings spilled onto the crushed white sprays, and she retied the bag quickly so the floral fragrance couldn't escape. Let the contents molder together, as they deserved!

In the study, after breakfasting, she threw herself into cleaning a ghastly scene of brown bovines clustered under a tree, a painting that would be as deathly dull once cleaned as it was right now. She'd been avoiding the painting, worst of the lot she'd brought from New York, simply because she hated it so much. Her feelings were only partly vented by the mineral spirits attacking its outer layer of grime.

"Just the same as your mind, Seth Whitlaw," she whispered grimly, daubing away some tobacco-colored muck. "Clean off the top layer, and what do you find? More muck!"

But, much as she might want to, she couldn't vent her viciousness on the canvas itself, so she was still in an evil frame of mind in midmorning, when her front doorbell rang.

By then she was working with stronger solvents. She couldn't walk away and leave them on the canvas, so before going to the door she patiently started to swab the tiny patch she was working on with turpentine, although the penetration of varnish was not quite complete, in order to stop the solvent's action. The doorbell rang again and no feet came through, so she knew it was neither of the Merriweather sisters.

She looked up, exasperated. Surely Seth wouldn't dare show his face at her door after what he'd implied! But she thought it must be he, for she'd heard no cars nearby for the past hour or so, and the Three Widows were too removed from the main road to attract foot traffic.

A polite, insistent knock followed the two rings, but still Danny didn't hurry. Before she answered, she picked up the bottle of turpentine and sprinkled the smelly liquid liberally over her smock. For good measure, as she walked to the door, she mussed her hair. Let no man dare say she was trying to attract him!

The icy antagonism in her eyes had been put there for Seth, but it was not Seth at the door. It was Jesse Horowitz, looking mildly friendly, with a guarded smile sandwiched between his beard and his mustache. Danielle's expression didn't alter a whit. He was Seth's man, and therefore tarred with the same brush.

He had a flat cardboard box in his arms, the size of a large dress box, and she wondered if it was a peace offering. A small mink, perhaps? She'd as soon accept a skinned skunk.

"Yes?" she said coldly.

"I've brought the Watteau, Mrs. Morrow," Jesse said. "Er . . . by the way, I don't think your door-bell's working."

Danny had forgotten about the canvas. It was on the tip of her tongue to tell Jesse Horowitz to take his business—*Seth's* business—elsewhere. She stood for a moment, thinking, her face masked with pride. So Seth thought she'd still deal with him, did he? Well, she'd see about that.

"Come in, Mr. Horowitz," she said crisply. "First we have to discuss terms, contracts and so forth. I'm sure Mr. Whitlaw doesn't want to get into this without knowing my exact fee. I should hate to become involved in a wrangle about overcharging."

Jesse's face was bland. "Naturally," he said smoothly. "I had intended to ask for a quote."

She stood aside as he entered, then turned and led him to the study. At this point, she didn't give a fig whether he saw the Sargent or not. If he asked questions, she'd tell him it was none of his business.

Jesse trailed her warily, recognizing the signs of an adversary worth being wary about. In the study he looked about with interest while Danny unpacked the Watteau. That done, she left him standing on his feet while she sat down, pulling the microscope into place so she could examine the painting.

Inside its elaborate frame, the Watteau was badly darkened and in very poor condition, eighteenth-century shepherdesses dancing in a ring. It was quite large for a Watteau, about eighteen by twenty-four inches. Danny pretended to examine each square inch in detail. In truth she wasn't even seeing through the lens, because she wasn't interested in a painting she didn't want to work on. Her eyes, while purportedly trained downward, were watching the restless shifting of Jesse Horowitz's legs with growing satisfaction. He stood in front of the Sargent for a while, but then he moved away to the window, and she knew he was growing impatient.

She stuck to her inspection and once in a while pretended to make a notation on a pad at her elbow. She measured the painting carefully. She ostentatiously consulted some reference books.

She kept him waiting for nearly an hour, because she knew that meant keeping Seth waiting too. Finally she raised her head, smiling pleasantly. "Naturally, it's insured?"

"Naturally."

"May I ask for how much? I sometimes base my fee on a percentage of value."

"Three hundred thousand."

"Fine. If Mr. Whitlaw agrees to my terms, he'll have to sign a contract agreeing to let me proceed. It's a standard form. In this case, because of the value of the work, I want his signature notarized."

"I . . . imagine that can be arranged. Er . . . by the way, Mr. Whitlaw asked me to tell you that if he *is* satisfied with your work, there are a number of other old paintings he might entrust to you. You might want to consider that in your quote."

"I'm sorry, no cut rates for quantity. You understand, this sort of work is very painstaking, especially on a painting nearly three centuries old. It's in very bad condition. The surface is badly crackled and I detect traces of mold—have you been storing it in a humid, dark room that doesn't get aired very often? Also, the canvas is sure to need relining because it's badly decayed. That's a highly delicate, specialized operation. The whole thing is going to take months, and I have to charge a fair price for my time. Payment in advance, by certified check only. I refuse to handle cash. And if Mr. Whitlaw thinks my quote too high, he'll have to try elsewhere. I might even be able to suggest where he can go.''

"And the quote, Mrs. Morrow . . . ?''

"Two cents,'' she said calmly, "but you can tell Mr. Whitlaw I'm worth it.''

When Jesse Horowitz left Middle Widow, his face was a study.

"Two *cents!*'' Seth shouted at Jesse. "The hell I'll pay two cents! If I tried to certify a check for that, they'd laugh me out of the bank!''

"I'm only repeating her terms,'' Jesse said mildly. In one hand he held the Watteau, which Danielle had insisted on returning until a firm agreement was reached. In the other hand he held her quote, in writing, ready for Seth's signature.

Seth glowered. His temper, normally even, had been driven to pressure-cooker point. He'd spent most of the night pacing the floor of his bedroom at East Widow—alternately burning up with desire, frustration, feelings of impotence, and reluctant admiration for the woman next door. He had the vague notion that he hadn't handled Danielle very well on the beach, but try as he might, he had been able to think of no way in which he would have handled her differently.

And now impotent rage was the strongest of his feelings, for he was wondering how in hell she kept managing to get the better of him.

"She's only bluffing because she doesn't want to do the job!"

"My impression exactly. She's clever, Seth. I don't know what her game is, but—"

"Well, this time I'm well ahead of you, friend! Because I *do!*"

In a matter of seconds Seth strode to the front entrance of Middle Widow and banged furiously on the door, the punishment to his fist giving some small release to his feelings. His other hand leaned on the doorbell.

"Open the hell up!" he shouted at the top of his lungs, rattling the handle. In anticipation of his possible arrival, Danielle had locked the door. She took her sweet time, and one of the Merriweather windows had flown open long before she reached the front of the house.

"Yes?" she said. Her knees might be quivering, but to outward appearances butter wouldn't have melted in her mouth. The strong fumes of turpentine enveloped her in invisible armor, and since Jesse's departure, she had wiped a streak of grime onto her face.

Seth almost pushed his way into the hall. Once inside, he slammed the door behind him. He stood and faced her, arms akimbo, brow like lightning, face like a stormcloud. The gentle giant had turned into a very angry one. "What the hell d'you mean, pulling a stunt like this?"

The arch of Danielle's brow was delicate. "Are you suggesting I've overpriced myself, Mr. Whitlaw? Perhaps you think I should give you a special rate because of favors already rendered? Sorry. Flowers and champagne picnics don't cut a whole lot of ice with me. I won't come down a single penny."

Through his teeth Seth gritted, "If you think you're going to force me into something . . ."

Her gaze trickled coolly over him, from the top of his lion-colored head to the soles of his bare feet. In between, old gold cords and a white turtleneck did little to hide the structure of hard musculature. Tall though Danny was, he towered over her, and his powerful physique made a mockery of her calm defiance.

"Force? I never force unwilling men, Mr. Whitlaw. It's against my principles to take advantage of the weaker sex."

Seth grabbed her by the upper arms and gave her a sharp shake. "Don't play with words!" he thundered. "Now stop this crap and name your price."

Danny managed to remain aloof, although his directness felt like another brutal body blow below the belt, for she didn't think he was referring to the Watteau. Anger stiffened her backbone, and although her arms felt like custard where he clutched them, her heart felt like granite. "I already did name it. My rates and terms haven't changed since Mr. Horowitz relayed the information. If they're not satisfactory, you can—" She bit back the expression "go to hell," which was not in keeping with the distance she wanted to maintain. "You can take your dirty pictures elsewhere."

It enraged Seth that she had kept her cool while he lost his. He made a strangled sound as he swallowed his impotent fury, and it was only with a great exertion of willpower that he kept his fingers from biting deeply into her arms. Instead, he bit out with words. "I know damn well what you're trying to do, Danielle Morrow. Well, as far as I'm concerned you can wait till hell freezes over!"

"As far as you're concerned, I had intended to," she said with admirable loftiness.

A dull brick color started to suffuse Seth's face. His eyes narrowed with the frustrations of dealing with a woman not quite like any other in his experience. At the moment he felt that even his wife had been preferable. At least she hadn't been so quick with her tongue.

His voice lowered to a furious hiss. "Enough of these silly preliminaries. You wouldn't give a crazy quote like that unless you had something quite different in mind. Perhaps an attempt to get back to me, after you'd used the wrong tactics last night? Well, I've decided I will deal with you, after all. So let's drop the nonsense and get down to business."

Her smile became a trifle fixed. "Not without a certified check. You'll also have to sign the quote and the release form I gave Mr. Horowitz. Didn't he explain?"

"Dammit, Danielle, you know bloody well we're not talking about a picture! And we're not talking about two cents!"

"What are we talking about, then? One red one?"

"Stop being mulish!" He glared at her. "Are you going to let me become your lover," he demanded harshly, "or are you not?"

"That depends," Danny said coolly.

Seth's face softened, and she could see the temporary, triumphant satisfaction gleaming in his face, along with a return of faint scorn. He relaxed a little, the confident male victor thinking he had won. Then his eyes narrowed cautiously. "Depends on what?"

She looked at him steadily, well bolstered by the nerve that had once seen her through several hair-raising months of market speculation. "On your price. Better keep it low, Mr. Whitlaw. Other women may think you're worth one cent, but personally, I wouldn't pay a tenth of that."

Seth reacted out of rage and frustration. His face descended with punishing swiftness, and he pried her lips apart, trying to plunder what Danny fully intended to withhold from him. Today she was angry enough to do so. She remained stiff in his arms, submitting when he bent her like a reed, but only because his superior strength forced her to submit. There was rejection in every rigid muscle of her body, and her mind was walled against him.

Her lack of response reached Seth. With a groan he released her, angry at her, even angrier at himself for trying to take by storm what he hadn't been able to get for himself by other means. He glowered at her furiously, jaw muscles trying to work out his rage. "You're too damn clever with your tongue, Danielle Morrow, and I don't trust clever women. Be warned— I'm on my guard. So whatever you have up your sleeve, don't bother trying it out."

Danny's eyes grew as cool as green-tinged icicles in winter. The only thing up her sleeve was her own arm, and at this moment in time she would very, very much like to have tried it out. Never before in her life had she wanted to punch anyone, but there was a first for everything.

"You'd better go," she said quietly. "I don't think we can do business."

She went and opened the door for him and stood with a stony expression, staring directly ahead, not looking at him. She wanted to weep with vexation and a thousand other emotions, and she was desperate for him to leave.

"Damn right we can't," Seth clipped after a minute. "But you'll come around in time. Let me know when you're ready to stop these wretched pennywhistle games and start talking *real* sense."

He strode through the door without even looking at her, while Danny restrained herself from retorting angrily that she already had.

"And happy birthday, dammit," he growled as he went past her.

Another delivery van arrived shortly thereafter. Danny moved out into the sunshine on the small open front stoop, because by this point there would be no avoiding neighborly curiosity anyway. After the way Seth had banged at her door a short time before, there were sure to be probing questions.

Several elegant boxes emerged from the van's hold. With the first of these in her arms, Danny recognized the discreet logo of a very exclusive, very expensive Boston shop. "You'd better wait," she warned the delivery man. "I believe there's some mistake. I don't think these are for me."

"They better be," the man grumbled. "Never in my life had to make a delivery this far afield. Special trip, this is. If I go back with the lot, I'll be in hot water."

She instructed him to stack the boxes on her steps while she opened the topmost out in full view. She hoped Seth was looking too.

The man shuffled through papers, consulting his instructions. "Three Widows, Nantucket . . . I could have sworn I came to the right place."

"Sounds right. But wait and I'll tell you for sure," Danny advised, lifting her brows as she uncovered a decidedly naughty black nightie.

Two boxes later, she found a small card that came nestled in the tissue. *Good morning, darling,* it read. *Thank you for last night. May there be many more like it, all of them in my arms.* Anger balled in her stomach like a fist. She knew the card must have been written a few days before. It wasn't even in Seth's handwriting, which she had seen on the florist's card, and she realized he must have had to make the arrangements by phone. So he had been that sure of success, had he?

Danny pulled the sheerest of filmy negligees from its tissue paper wrappings and held it against herself, so the odor of turpentine would cling to it. "Very sexy," she admired, drawing the delivery man's eyes. She knew he would not be the only person looking. "All the same, it's not for me."

He scratched his head. "The name isn't Morrow?"

Danny ostentatiously dropped the negligee into its box with two fingers, as if it were a soiled handker chief. She pointed at East Widow. "That's the house you want," she said disapprovingly. "Unless you're good at dodging passes, take my advice. Just drop the whole pile at his door without ringing, and run as fast as you can. The bachelor who lives in there has an underwear fetish, and you never know *what* he's going to be wearing when he answers."

"Rattling doors," Mildred snorted as she cut the birthday cake. "Shouting. Sending truckloads of sinful things. Good thing you sent that scoundrel packing."

"Flowers don't seem so very sinful to me," Emma said wistfully. "Not that you should encourage him even the tiniest mite, Danny, but it *is* very romantic. . . ."

"Hmmph!" Mildred handed the first slice of cake to Danielle. "Nothing romantic about the primrose path, when it leads to hellfire and brimstone. And what's he going to do with those shameful unmentionables now? Hang them on some other scarlet woman, like that showgirl he used to have?"

"Probably," Danielle said unenthusiastically.

"She wasn't a showgirl, Mil," Emma quavered. "She was an actress. She even did some Shakespeare."

"Same difference," Mildred said tartly. She turned to Danny. "I'm glad to learn, young missie, that you've got more moral stuffing now than you had when you were a girl." She had never quite forgiven her one-time charge for being pregnant at the time of her wedding. "The way that Roger Morrow swept you off your feet, I'd given you up as a bad job."

"I've learned a thing or two since then," Danny murmured. The anger that had kept her going earlier in the day seemed very elusive now. She was feeling extremely depressed and trying to hide it. With hindsight, she had begun to regret some of her dramatic gestures. It would have been better to react with cool indifference, making no gestures at all.

Somehow she managed to get through the evening, soothing Emma when she became fluttery and superstitious, reassuring Mildred that no amount of pressure from Seth Whitlaw would cause her to weaken. It was still early, not long past dark, when Danny escaped West Widow with its antimacassars, its petit-point chairs, its horsehair-stuffed sofas—and its overflow of Seth's flowers.

She kissed both the Merriweather maidens good night and said a last thank-you for her birthday presents, which had become a tradition over the years. Always, there would be a wall sampler embroidered with a moral message from Mildred, and from Emma some pretty satin sachets, fragrantly feminine, hand-made with herbs or flowers Emma grew herself. Danny was relieved that this year the latter smelled of lavender, not lily of the valley, as had the previous year's offering.

Her footsteps dragged as she approached Middle Widow. She felt enormously weary, and she was experiencing some of the shakiness she had been too numb to feel the night before. She was glad to see that the lingerie boxes had not been stacked at her door during her absence, as she had half feared. She entered her home, grateful that the overpowering aura of flowers was at last leaving it.

Upstairs, her bedroom was well aired. It was a little messy, though. The previous evening she had dragged a blanket off the bed for use elsewhere, and she had thrown her dress—the dress she'd worn to the beach— over a chair. Reluctantly she went to it, knowing that Seth's tiny nosegay was still pinned to the fabric. One last thing to get rid of. She felt she had the strength to do that, and no more.

The flowers were wilted and yellowed by now, and Danny held her breath while her fingers searched for the pin that held them in place. It was elusive at first, concealed by the nosegay. And then her fingers connected with something that didn't feel quite right. Unlike most corsage pins, this one had a round knob at the sharp end, a safety device to prevent puncturing. . . or maybe loss. . . .

Suddenly she was wrenching at the flowers, at that moment not caring if she ripped the dress. She was filled with a sickening sensation, knowing quite well what was coming. The pin, well secured to the fabric, stayed put, but gave up its floral concealment. Danny stared as anger washed over her in waves, each higher than the wave it succeeded. It was only a discreet stickpin, the sort that might be used to anchor a scarf, but real gold was real gold. And she didn't need a jeweler's loupe to know that the one enormous emerald on its head was genuine.

So that was why Seth still refused to believe she wasn't a mercenary bitch! He would naturally expect her to have made this discovery after leaving him the

night before. No doubt, he thought she'd accepted his
one truly valuable gift—no, bribe—and was holding
out only because it wasn't enough.

   Sparkling with renewed strength, her eyes lifted in
the direction of East Widow. She did indeed have one
more thing to get rid of, and it wouldn't wait till
morning.

Chapter Seven

*Y*ou were right, Seth, it is the Morrow woman at the door," Jesse informed his employer. "I showed her into your living room."

Seth looked up from the book he had been pretending to read, or rather burying his frustrations in. "And what frame of mind does she appear to be in tonight?" he asked sarcastically. He himself was not in a particularly good one, but at least he was in control as he hadn't been earlier in the day. At Danielle's arrival, he had not moved from the upstairs TV room of East Widow, nor had he made any effort to change out of his old cords, old sweater, and old sneakers. He was damned if he'd put himself out for a woman whose main recreation was trading insults, especially as he was half convinced that she was only another edition of his unscrupulous ex-wife.

Jesse made his meticulous observations. "I can't tell

you what's going on in her head, Seth, but to outward appearances I'd have to say she's softening. She's wearing makeup and perfume and she's dressed in some long, creamy caftan thing she certainly didn't wear to the Merriweathers'. And she's all charm. I must confess I'm a bit surprised.''

Seth's face reflected some grim satisfaction. ''I'm not.'' He snapped his book closed and put it aside. ''She must have found the emerald.''

''She certainly must have. She was wearing it at her throat.''

A slow smile spread over Seth's face, and at last he rose to his feet. ''Well, now,'' he drawled. ''That's the sort of news a man likes to hear. I guess she's about to show her true colors. Go pour her a drink, will you, Jesse? Tell her I was asleep but that I'll be down in a few minutes.''

Jesse hesitated. ''I don't think she's the type of woman who wants to be kept waiting, Seth.''

Seth laughed softly. ''She'll wait,'' he predicted confidently, all good temper restored. ''The shoe's on the other foot now, isn't it?''

Jesse shuffled uncomfortably. ''I have to confess, Seth. I'm not so sure it is. Personally, I'm beginning to think I may have been altogether wrong about the Morrow woman. What if she's not after your money? I haven't told you about this yet, but she owns a huge Sargent portrait, one of her ancestors I presume. What if she once owned other works of art? What if she came by some money that way? Or some other way we don't know about? She's clever, Seth, and not only with her tongue. If you'd seen the look that delivery man gave me when I went to open the door this morning . . .''

Seth was on his way out of the room, but he paused long enough to give his assistant an exasperated glance. "This is one helluva time to decide she's not a gold digger, Jesse. Just when she's about to prove that she *is*."

"Is she?" Jesse rubbed his beard ruefully. "At this point, until she's made her next move, I don't know what to make of her. And neither should you."

As Seth strode for his bedroom, he flung a few impatient words over his shoulder. "Oh, for God's sake, Jesse. Don't *you* fall in love with her too."

Jesse stared after his boss, wondering if he realized what he had confessed to.

Danny didn't mind the wait, which gave her a chance to think over the coming encounter. She fingered the emerald at her throat gingerly while she sipped the gin and tonic Jesse Horowitz had brought her. She was not so unsubtle as to use the stickpin in the way she felt Seth deserved, but she did intend to deflate a little of his ego with it.

The luxurious caftan she wore was one she'd owned for a long time; it had been part of her bridal trousseau many years before. Wearing it had a dual purpose. First, she was perfectly aware of the vision she presented in heavy, embroidered old-ivory satin that flowed around her body slowly, like thick honey, whenever she moved; second, she knew she wouldn't forget herself while wearing something that reminded her of her late husband.

Seth arrived in the living room ostensibly smothering a yawn. His hair was tousled, and he wore a black cotton kimono. The gold-colored pant legs protruding from beneath its hem were not those of his cords. "Sorry," he muttered sleepily. "Had to find me a pair of decent pajamas. Don't use 'em, normally."

Danny didn't rise to her feet. Were Seth's words supposed to conjure up disturbing visions of naked flesh? They did; but at the moment the heating thought only fueled her well-hidden anger. Her lashes drooped in a curtain, sweeping her cheeks, veiling her thoughts.

"What *do* you normally sleep in, Mr. Whitlaw?" she asked in a pleasant, husky voice. She knew she had to be clever enough to let the first move come from him.

Seth chuckled, and the chuckle ended in another yawn. "Is that idle curiosity, or concerned interest?"

"Concerned interest."

Seth moved slowly closer, but only circled her chair, a predator stalking the prey that was almost his, pretending only minimal interest. He knew he had to be clever enough to let the first move come from her.

"May I ask why the concern?"

Danielle smiled a cool, slightly distant smile. "Why, sleeping in your skin, Mr. Whitlaw, you might catch a chill. I should hate to think you were a . . . cold man."

Just out of range of her vision, Seth's eyes narrowed. Throw his own words in his teeth, would she? Incautiously he growled, "That's a fine challenge to fling in the face of a hot-blooded seadog like me, Madame Morrow. No other woman has ever found cause to complain about my body temperature."

Danielle turned in her chair to look at him directly, her face very serious. "Really? I find that hard to believe. What do they complain about?"

"Nothing," Seth snapped, and then forced himself to simmer back to patience. He could feel the small hairs on the nape of his neck prickle in a primitive, silent warning. Was she not finished with her games, then? How long did she intend to keep playing cat-and-mouse with him? And dammit, who was the cat and who was the mouse?

Danielle just sat placidly, sipping her drink, aware that she had scored a small victory. Seth was already off balance.

"I'm glad to see you're enjoying your birthday present," he observed tersely.

Danny smiled, letting her eyes soften. "I came over to thank you for it, Seth. It's a beautiful . . ." She paused delicately ". . . trinket."

Seth had moved directly in front of her chair. Once more in command, he had schooled his reactions. His mouth was impassive, subtly hardened, the eyes very watchful behind their hooded lids. A *trinket?* From Van Cleef & Arpels? She was telling him, and not too subtly, that it hadn't been enough. "I take it you didn't know about the emerald until a few minutes ago," he observed sardonically.

"No," she said, fingering her throat in a gesture that was protective and provocative all at once. Her eyes held to Seth's. She added huskily, "And I'm truly, truly sorry for that. If I'd known . . ."

A controlled smile gradually took possession of Seth's hard mouth. He had her now. "Someday you must tell me about your taste in . . . trinkets."

Arrogant bastard, she thought, hearing the undercurrent of faint contempt in his voice. So he put her in the category of his easy showgirls, did he? She manufactured a light, husky, sophisticated laugh that contained a wealth of suggestiveness.

"Someday I'll tell you . . . *every*thing I like," she murmured, "and you must tell me too." She uttered the words slowly so that their nuances hung in the air.

Holding Seth's eyes all the while, she allowed her mouth to part invitingly. She lifted her glass, even though it was now empty but for ice. She touched her tonguetip to the chilled contents. Then, lowering her glass and still watching him, she used the cold tongue-tip to caress the very center of her upper lip. The drawn-out, seductive gesture promised a wealth of earthly pleasures without a single word spoken.

Seth's eyes started to glaze and darken, and she saw the desire growing in his face, turning his mouth sensuous and heavy with wanting. In the silence of the room, she heard his breathing grow heavier. From the unsmiling, hungry way he was looking at her, she knew he must be envisioning to himself the act of possession, imagining the prize now easily within his reach.

Danny allowed him lots of time to imagine, repeating her small performance with the lower lip. Again, she didn't take her eyes off Seth. He could hardly miss her meaning.

He was still standing in front of her chair, towering over her. Fancying himself in the masterful, dominant position, she supposed. Well, it was time to start puncturing his pride. She put down the emptied glass she had been toying with and rose gracefully to her feet. She summoned a small, cool, distant smile to her lips. "I must go now. Thanks for the drink, Mr. Whitlaw, and—"

"The hell you'll go," he muttered harshly, the edge of desire deepening his voice. He seized her upper arms and pulled her hard against his kimono, so that she became at once aware of the stirrings she had aroused. His eyes smoldered down at her, the fires of anger hidden within the smoke of desire. "Don't tell me you don't know exactly what you were implying with that wicked little performance. I don't like women who make promises they're not prepared to keep."

"Promises, Mr. Whitlaw?" Danny hid her trembling, for she knew she had to be the ice maiden once more. She steeled herself to go through with the last part of her performance. "I promised nothing . . . *you* promised nothing. . . ."

The words trailed away, their meaning clear. Seth fought to control his frustrated passion, but it was a losing battle. The need for Danielle, which had been consuming his dreams and his days, had become volcanic. Damn her anyway! She knew precisely what she had been doing with her tongue, and he hated her for the erotic stimulation . . . hated her and wanted her. The feel of her willowy body clamped against his, not resisting but not encouraging, was enough to send his caution flying to the winds.

"I'll make it worth your while, I promise," he muttered thickly. He bent to devour the taste of her skin, and although her hands remained between them, pressing against his chest, she didn't try to avoid his burning kisses. His open mouth dropped an impassioned trail over her neck, her eyelids, her ears, and all the while he muttered his rash promises. "Jewels, furs . . . oh God, I want you . . . a Rolls, if you must . . . I must have you . . . let me love you, Danielle. Be my mistress, darling. You won't regret it, I promise. You'll never work again, as long as you're mine . . . a penthouse, anything . . . as long as you're *mine*. . . ."

Danny closed her eyes and shuddered beneath the sensuous, siren magic of his kisses, but the words were enough to keep her cool head in control. She permitted, but without active response.

When none of his blandishments produced a return of ardor, Seth at last grew still. Not releasing Danielle, he drew apart enough that he could see her face. Desire had become such a burning, immediate thing that it consumed the last shreds of reason. He wound one hand into her hair, while the fingers of his other hand dropped urgently lower to mold the satin swell over her breasts. "Name it, then," he muttered unwisely, fiercely.

Danny breathed slowly, trying to transcend the power of passion. She didn't push his possessive hand away, because she knew the feel of her aroused nipple would encourage him. Considering the fluid state of her limbs, her faint smile was a masterpiece. She hoped it looked acquisitive. "I've already told you my terms, Seth," she breathed softly. "Please don't touch . . . not yet."

His eyes questioned her, and his mouth grew pained with the effort, but reluctantly he removed his hand from her breast. Even more slowly, with his jaw reflecting the difficulty of control, he withdrew his fingers from her hair.

It was her turn to touch. Her fingers trailed skillfully downward, lingering on his chest and stomach lightly, arousingly. "Did you think my silly offer to Jesse was only a joke? I *was* talking sense, Seth . . . common sense. In advance, certified . . .''

Seth stiffened and his mouth thinned. No woman, not even his wife, had ever asked him outright for money, and he disliked the connotations. It took him a moment to fight his inner battles. "How much?" he demanded harshly.

Danny pretended to think. Her hands slid around his waist, suggestively stroking his hips, stoking his fires as she worked her way around, at last locking her fingers behind him. She held the upper half of her body a little apart, but pressed her thighs against him until he could not stifle a groan. His hardness was a sensory stimulant she would remember later in the sanctuary of her own bed, but for the moment Danielle held to thoughts of her anger and guarded her natural reactions. Seth gritted his teeth and closed his eyes, visible evidence of the battle he was fighting. She rubbed herself against him just long enough to be certain he would lose it.

"I'm sure I can leave that to you," she said softly, at last breaking the close contact. She had no idea what would sound outrageous to Seth, and she had concluded that it was best to let his imagination do the deciding. "But remember, I'm not easily . . . convinced."

Seth's tormented eyes came open. He was shuddering. "You can't leave now," he said thickly. "You can't. Not now, not like this."

"You haven't convinced me yet," Danny murmured, easing gradually away from him.

Seth's eyes flared with sudden open contempt, and he managed to pull himself completely apart. "I will," he said tightly, and hated himself for saying it. "Monday morning, as soon as the banks are open."

Danny tilted her head coquettishly. "Is that a certified promise?"

"I am a man of my word," Seth clipped.

Danny tiptoed up and touched her tonguetip to his chin, rubbing it erotically as she had earlier rubbed it on ice. "This is a taste of what's to come," she whispered as she dampened his skin. "I'm sure you'll be generous enough to please me, Seth."

This time Seth remained hard as a rock, fortified by disgust at himself. "Is that so I'll spend the weekend remembering you're not . . . cheap?" His tone suggested the opposite.

"Exactly," she murmured. She couldn't have put it better herself. She backed away from Seth and gave him the smile of a contented cat. "Don't bother coming to the door, Seth. I'll show myself out."

With eyes now watchfully narrowed, he allowed her to go.

"Danielle."

His quiet voice stopped her just before she reached the door, and she turned, holding a protective hand to her throat. She was gripped with a deep sense of unease because she wondered if she had been congratulating herself too soon.

The message in Seth's eyes seemed to rip holes in her, and at that moment, forgetting all her very worthy motives, she did feel cheap. Very, very cheap indeed.

"When I'm buying," he said scornfully, with his gaze trickling from top to toe, "I expect a better good night kiss than that. Get back here, Danielle, and kiss me properly, or when I'm writing that check I might forget a zero or two.''

Danny could feel some of the blood draining from her cheeks, for the evening's performance was not over until she was safely home. Much as instinct attracted her to Seth Whitlaw physically, she disliked kissing a man who treated her as he might treat an overpriced call girl.

Stay cool, she reminded herself. *Stay cool.*

She walked back across the room and into his arms. She steeled herself, for she expected Seth's kiss to be demanding and contemptuously possessive, the unfeeling kiss of a man taking something for which he was paying dearly.

It was not like that at all, except for the first slow eternity when he kept her waiting. Without urgency, watching her all the while, he wound the long hank of her hair around a hand to position her for the kiss.

But then his lips descended gently, asking rather than claiming, promising in the most seductive way that he was going to be a very, very good lover indeed. He wooed her with tender nibbles, with a softly exploring tongue, and in the end it was Danny who moaned and parted widely, and reached around Seth's neck to hold his head more closely, hungrily seeking even more than he had given. Lost in the moist depths of his mouth, she offered something she had intended to withhold—a true measure of her passionate nature.

She was dazed when Seth broke the kiss, which had deepened into ardent intimacy. He set her apart, although his breath was unsteady and his eyes were darkened with desire.

"And that's certified too," he murmured. Danny stared at him for a minute and then fled East Widow, far less gracefully than she had intended to.

In her own home, in her safe, well-aired bedroom, she was trembling with unruly feelings as she flung off her clothes. The kiss had very nearly melted the core of her hardened heart, and the various influences she'd been suppressing for twenty-four hours now assailed her like many enemies attacking at once, from all sides. Subliminal images kept surfacing, each small vision a weapon against her will. She closed her eyes and fought them.

Seth's amber-flecked eyes with their intriguing laughter lines. His wonderful, piratical eyebrows. His strong, sensuous mouth. His big-boned frame. His large, capable hands. His tenderness. His fierceness. His sense of humor. His kindness to a young girl in a shop. His sexuality. His . . . maleness. His nakedness of the night before.

She thought of the moon turning to gold where it had traced the deep bronze of his muscled arms and legs, and to silver where it had outlined the pale, hard, intimate skin surfaces protected by his bathing suit. At the time, she hadn't even known she'd been so utterly aware of those things. Now they were like mind pictures, flashing their potent images in her brain.

And his taste, still on her tongue . . .

Still in her undergarments, she raced to the bathroom and cleaned her teeth and rinsed with antiseptic mouthwash and then pressed her hands against her eyes, ordering them to stop remembering.

Finally calming a little, she made her way to bed. She donned one of the oversize T-shirts she always slept in, refusing to look at her own body because she was angry at it for betraying her so badly. She turned off the light and climbed into bed, vowing that she would exorcise Seth Whitlaw from her head if she had to beat it against a wall.

After a few minutes of staring at the darkened ceiling, trying not to think of the man next door—sleeping naked, she remembered in a rush—she turned onto one side and angrily punched her pillow into shape. "Take that! And that! And that!" she cried. "And don't ever insult me again!"

The exercise ended when her face buried itself in the pillow, simply to stifle the sobs she didn't want to waste on Seth Whitlaw. And that was when her fingers connected with something under the pillow. One last, tiny memento of him that she'd forgotten to remove.

She pulled the crushed stem of lily of the valley from its hiding place, intending to hurl it across the room. Instead, she found herself bathing it with passionate tears, the tiny, fragrant spray pressed to her lips.

Hard as it was to exorcise Seth from her head, it was going to be even harder to exorcise him from her heart.

Next door, Seth was still up. Since Danny's departure, he had been prowling the living room like a caged lion, occasionally stopping to bang his hand forcefully against a wall. Grimly, he wondered why he felt so little exultation, when he was now assured of success. Danielle's hefty demands were not the reason for his disturbance. That was strong medicine, but he'd made the decision that he would have to swallow it.

He was upset because . . . he didn't know why he was upset. He supposed it was because she had kissed to order, unleashing passion only after the cold-blooded arrangements were made.

Jesse arrived with a tray, and at last Seth stopped his restless pacing. Seeing the brandy bottle and glass he'd asked for, he calmed. Jesse placed the tray on a sideboard and poured a snifter, which he carried to his employer. "Anything else?" he asked.

"No," Seth said between his teeth. "I've got everything I want now, haven't I?"

"So it seems," Jesse replied stiffly, his face impassive.

Seth raised his glass and quaffed it in a single draft. "Salud, friend. You'd better get off to bed, because I'm about to settle into some serious celebrating."

Jesse merely stood there, his lips clamped tight.

Seth wiped his mouth, staring in unfriendly fashion. "Don't look so damn disapproving. You know I never get drunk. Tonight I deserve it. This has been a helluvan expensive day." He yanked the sash of his kimono tighter to signal his determination and swiveled sharply away to the sideboard.

He put down the snifter, picked up the whole brandy bottle, and started toward the couch. He stopped and glowered at his man, who still stood like a poker at the door. "One Mildred Merriweather is enough for this neck of the woods," he said tightly. "My God! Nothing as righteous as a reformed alcoholic. What the hell are you standing there for?"

"To make sure you don't sit down." Jesse's face was suspiciously straight. "There's something sticking into the back of your dressing gown, Seth, in a very vital spot. Er . . . may I venture the guess that it's an emerald, attached to a gold pin?"

Chapter Eight

For the first time in days, Danny missed her dawn swim. Conquering superstitious fears no longer seemed as important as conquering herself. In the morning she stood for a long time, looking at the face of the other Danielle in the Sargent portrait. Since youth, she had studied that face so often, seeing the mirror of her own features, that the portrait seemed almost like an alter ego. Danny knew that Emma with her superstitious twaddle, and even Mildred with her dire warnings and her vague hints of reincarnation, had encouraged the belief. It was partly for this reason, an irrational one admittedly, that Danny had not been able to sell the portrait years before.

Untouched, untouchable let her be

"I think you were a courageous woman," Danny whispered. "You loved Jethro, and when they took him away from you by creating that curse, you did what you had to do. It was pride that made you undress on the beach that day, wasn't it? You weren't cheap, but in your grief and anger you didn't care what anybody thought. You were only showing the world that you had loved your man, weren't you? I wish I were as brave as you. But I'm not . . . brave. You see, the other night I was on a beach too. And I didn't even have the courage to show *one person.* If I'd had the guts to give him my love right then, I wouldn't be in this mess today. But I didn't show him, because . . .''

Or lie ten fathom under

"And I still can't show him," Danny whispered, burying her face in her hands. "There's nothing to it, I know, but what if Seth . . . and he does go to sea, all the time . . . and . . . oh, God, if it hadn't been for Roger I'd never *believe* in this wretched nonsense."

At last Danny turned away. Overnight, as testified by the dark circles under her eyes, she had accepted one thing. She loved Seth. It wasn't a passing thing; surely the years had proved that she didn't bestow her affections lightly. In the short course of her marriage, she had swiftly become aware of the difference between sexual attraction and love. Her husband had been a mature, magnetic man, charming in manner, adept in lovemaking. Danny had been very young and inexperienced, and he had swept her off her feet. From the first, Roger had urged marriage. Later, Danny wondered if his financial problems and the valuable Fielding property had influenced his thinking, but at the time that hadn't occurred to her. On learning of her pregnancy, she had very much wanted Roger's child, and she hadn't wanted it to be born a bastard. She had married, feeling herself too young to be tied, but thinking herself in love. Yet within weeks she had grown to know that Roger Morrow mastered only her body, not her heart.

Seth mastered both, and yet she could give him neither.

And after what she'd done to his pride, she didn't suppose he'd want any more to do with her, anyway. Dully, feeling as leaden as the overcast day outside, Danny went to her work table, but then remembered that she'd offered to drive the Merriweather sisters to church.

The occupation filled Danny's morning, and she realized that she didn't really want to be at home anyway, in case Seth showed up at her door. Not that he would. But if he did . . .

After that trick with the pin—even though the safety device had been firmly in place to prevent disaster—their next encounter was sure to be a nasty scene.

She spent the early part of her afternoon at the Merriweather house, weeding the rock garden for Emma until she could no longer bear to listen to Mildred's sermonizing about the short shorts and halter top she'd changed into. After that, Danny grabbed a sweater and sped off on her bike for a brisk pedal back into the town of Nantucket. As it was now the height of the tourist season and not a good day for the beach, the narrow streets were filled with strolling sightseers. She locked up her bike and became one of them, wandering aimlessly along the cobbled lanes and past the familiar silvery buildings of her youth, the stately old houses abutting the sidewalks in forthright fashion, proud and straight and simple as the settlers and seafarers who had built many of them.

Summer Street. India Street. Trader's Lane. Milk Street. She went by the Lydia Hinchman House, where Emma used to take her to see native plants and wildflowers when she was a child. Emma always used to whisper which growing things would ward off bad luck, which would help bring good weather, which should be tucked in the pocket to help cure stomach ache or sore feet or arthritis.

On Vestal Street, Danny passed the old jail. There were stocks and pillories in the jail yard, but she didn't enter to see. In her very early youth she had committed some minor offense, and Mildred had dragged her there by the ear to show her the wages of sin.

Main Street. Nodding occasionally at people she knew, Danny passed the Three Bricks—a trio of houses even better known in Nantucket than the Three Widows. Red brick buildings stood out on an island where even the big McDonald's restaurant, down by the boat basin in the harbor, served its hamburgers in a structure of weathered shingle, in keeping with the historic island architecture.

It was Danny's history, all of it. The old cobblestones that paved Main Street, and other streets in town, had probably arrived in Nantucket as ship's ballast. The very stones where she walked may have come in Fielding ships. Here and there along the sidewalks, children were selling sea shells and pretty stones. Danny stopped and bought a handful. She herself had done the same entrepreneurial thing as a youngster, the ''sin'' for which Mildred had taken her to see the pillories and the stocks.

Danny passed the old horse trough and dropped a penny in for good luck. Emma always used to do that.

She dropped the stones in too. Today Danny felt as if her past was a heavy, heavy heritage. Original sin and primitive superstition. At one point in her life she had put them both behind, only to have the dual influences come back to haunt her, both bolstered a thousandfold by the death of her husband and her own near drowning.

Danielle was no longer proud of her silly, smart little bits of vengeance the previous day. In particular, she had thoroughly repented her erotic suggestiveness. With her head cleared of anger, she knew that what she had done was an unforgivable thing to do to any man—no matter what had happened, no matter how much he had misinterpreted her motives, no matter how much he had insulted her. And to do that to a man she loved . . .

If there had ever been hope for a loving relationship with Seth Whitlaw, she had put paid to it, she believed, for once and for all. And all because she had been offended at his assumption that she would expect rewards for her favors. She ought to pity him if he expected that, because it meant that no woman had ever given him true, good love for himself and himself alone.

And if he had treated her like a whore the night

before, it was no more than she deserved. She had behaved like one. She felt shamed to remember her actions, all done from pique. Why hadn't she just dropped the emerald through his mailbox? That would have served as well. In hindsight, she realized that her motives for going through the seductive scene hardly bore examination.

Danny was too perturbed to remember hunger or watch the hour. She was still wandering through town at nine o'clock that evening, when the old Portuguese bell near the center of Nantucket town rang out its fifty-two peals, as it did three times each day. She looked up at the golden belfry, now darkened with the passage of sunset. The bell had been brought to Nantucket in 1830, the year of Jethro Fielding's birth. The custom of ringing it three times daily had started in 1849, the year when the first Danielle had been born in a great château, on an estate somewhere in Normandy.

It was a heavy heritage, indeed, but it was *her* heritage. Danny hated to think of it all coming to an end. Even if she did conquer all her doubts, at this point she could not imagine wanting to bear a child to any man but Seth, wanting to marry any man but Seth, wanting to make love to any man but Seth. And she was thirty years old: the birthday had given her another year, but it had taken one too.

The hourglass had turned again, the sands of time were running, and the future promised no man, no child, no love. Before the fifty-second bell peal sounded, Danny realized she was shivering.

Soon, with a bicycle light to guide her, she was on

the way home. As always, she rested at the top of the hill to look down upon the Three Widows.

She thought of Seth again, and she thought of the child she wanted so desperately, and unwillingly she saw that child as a small laughing-eyed pirate with Fielding blood, but with Seth's chin, eyes, tawny hair . . .

And that was when, with a small sense of shock, she saw Seth himself. Although he was no more than a dark shadow on her doorstep, dimly delineated because of a light somewhere in the house, she knew it was him. As she glided silently forward on her bike, she determined that he was sitting on the stoop, leaning against her door. She had the impression that he'd been there for hours. By the faint glow of her bike light, she saw his face and realized that he was asleep.

Because of the burglar alarm system, she couldn't get into her house without going past him. Entering through the rear, when the alarm was set, would trigger it. Quietly she put her bike away and walked to her front door, calling on the first Danielle Fielding to lend her courage and strength and dignity.

"Seth," she said quietly, and he woke on the instant. He hadn't actually moved, and in the dark she couldn't see his face, but she knew he was awake by the extra tension in the air, the sense of danger that infected her. "If you move aside, Seth, I'll open my door. Whatever you have to say, there's no need to say it in public."

Slowly Seth rose to his feet, a large looming shadow between Danielle and her front door. As levelly as if he had been awake all along, he said, "There's no need to say it in private, either. I have only three things to communicate, all of them very simple. First, I apologize wholeheartedly for underestimating you, Danielle Morrow."

Her satisfaction was fleeting, for Seth's next quiet words struck ice into her heart. "Second, if you think you're going to get out of your clever tuppenny quote, then you've got another think coming. I've got the quote in writing, remember. You signed the form you gave Jesse, and I'll be signing it too. I want that Watteau done, and I don't give a damn how many weeks or months it takes you or how much money you lose. Expect a certified check this week . . . and *then* let's see if you've got the guts to pretend you're not mercenary."

The habit of pride kept Danny silent, and darkness concealed the sting of tears in her eyes. She kept herself very straight and still and concentrated hard on conquering the lump in her throat.

"And third," Seth said in a tight, shaking voice, "don't think for a minute that I haven't figured out the real purpose of that pin-the-tail-on-the-donkey game. Oh, very clever, Danielle. Advertise your erotic talents, fill a man with frustrated desire, and at the same time demonstrate what a fine, upstanding woman you are. I should have known all along that you were playing for far higher stakes than I'd given you credit for."

Suddenly Seth's whole body was trembling with a hatred that chilled her to the bone. "If you expect to trick a proposal out of me, Danielle Morrow, go whistle in the wind. I'd die a single man, with no child to carry my name, before I'd marry another woman like my wife. Like *you*."

He stalked off into the night. Danny stared at his dark shape, frozen with the awfulness of what he had said. After her day of depression, no insult could have reached her more. She managed, just barely, to hold herself together long enough to enter her home.

Chapter Nine

𝒯he Watteau did indeed arrive back at Middle Widow several days later, carried by Jesse Horowitz. Danielle noticed the somewhat sheepish expression half-hidden in the wealth of black beard, but she studiously ignored it.

With a pale, determined face, and without comment, she accepted the picture, the signed agreement, and the certified check for two cents. Not wanting to overdramatize at this point, she didn't go through the gesture of ripping up the latter. That would be done later, in privacy—and not in anger, but in simple regret for all the mistakes and might-have-beens in her life.

"I won't be able to start this until I finish some other commissions," she advised Jesse. Her voice was dull, her eyes bleared with lack of sleep and too many hours spent in fine detail work. "I'll have to take it back to New York with me at the end of the summer."

"Fine. Er . . . may I come in?" he asked, when it appeared that Danny was about to close the door in his face.

"I don't think there's any need, Mr. Horowitz." She had checked inside the large box containing the painting. "Everything seems to be in order."

"Actually, I'd like to talk to you, Mrs. Morrow. To apologize."

Danny brushed a stray wisp of hair away from her forehead. "Apologize? There's no need for apologies. I wrote the quote; I'll do the job."

"My apology isn't as simple as that, because it involves a story. May I come in and tell it?" Jesse added persuasively, "Somehow, Mrs. Morrow, I don't think you're the type of woman who'd refuse to listen when a man admits his errors. I'm ready to admit mine."

He had hooked her, she had to admit. She looked at him uncertainly for a moment and then opened the door more fully. "Come in then, although it can't be for long. I have a lot of work to do. Would you like coffee? I have some on the hob. Go on in the living room and I'll bring you a cup."

"Might we sit in the study, Mrs. Morrow? I've been hoping to have another look at that fine portrait you own."

"Not today, if you don't mind. I'd like to get away from the clutter and the smell of solvents." She didn't add that she had been working flat out, sustaining herself on coffee and nerves and sheer grit, trying to accomplish as much of her paying work as possible before the Watteau arrived. If nothing else, it was an antidote to heartache. The effort had exhausted her, and although she had been denying her mind's and her body's tiredness, she needed a break.

Entering her living room with the coffee tray, she saw that Jesse Horowitz was wandering, having a look at the many antiques in the room. At that moment he was examining a glass-fronted case containing fine old brass sextants, an astrolabe, antique compasses, and other Fielding mementoes.

He remarked on some of them, then on the ancient grandfather's clock that told the phases of the moon. "I suppose these things have been in your family for generations," he commented, as he went to sit stiffly on a sofa that had started life as a captain's day bed. As always, he looked very proper and formal in a dark suit. "And the painting I saw the other day, of course. That intrigued me. You've sold all the rest of your family's art collection, have you?"

"There never was one."

Jesse started to ask more questions, but Danny didn't want to talk about the Fieldings. She handed Jesse a cup. "You had something to say to me," she reminded him.

"Er . . . it's a little hard to start, Mrs. Morrow. First I'd like to explain to you that I've been with the Whitlaw family for many, many years. I worked for Mr. Whitlaw senior when Seth was a boy. I was only a gentleman's gentleman then. However, over the years, I believe I've become more—personal assistant, secretary for Seth's most private concerns, and also his friend. I decided to speak to you today because I dislike having you think ill of my employer."

"Because he accepted my quote on the Watteau? I

don't think ill of him for that. If Mr. Whitlaw is taking advantage of a bargain, I have only myself to blame."

"That isn't the thrust of my story, Mrs. Morrow." Jesse looked at her squarely, his face very somber. "I have something else to explain. Believe me, I would never speak about my employer's personal concerns if I didn't think it was in his best interests. I was fond of the boy he used to be, Mrs. Morrow, and now I admire the man. I dislike seeing him make mistakes, especially when I myself must shoulder a responsibility for setting his feet on the wrong path."

"I'm not sure what you mean."

"I'm Seth's man, Mrs. Morrow, but I'm also his friend. When he was a young man, he trusted me, gave me a job after his father had fired me without references. You see, I was . . . *am* an alcoholic. Seth had faith in me, sobered me up, got me on my feet." Jesse paused. "He trusts me with the key to his liquor cabinet, Mrs. Morrow. I don't suppose you could know what that means to me, but I believe it's his trust that's kept me sober for years. I could never break it."

"Then perhaps you'd better not talk to me about this at all. My opinion of your employer isn't as poor as you seem to think."

Jesse leaned forward earnestly. "Actually," he said, "I wished to speak about his opinion of you."

He had hooked her again. Danielle could not deny the desire to hear what he had to say, and so she listened in silence as Jesse started speaking.

"My duties are many, as you probably know. Keeping my employer out of trouble is, I consider, one of them. I have to confess that I gave Seth a number of

bald facts that might tend to put you in a bad light. This
happened after my trip to New York, where I learned
that . . . but I'll come to that in time, Mrs. Morrow.
For the moment, suffice it to say that I looked into your
background in some detail, with the help of private
investigators. Mr. Whitlaw did ask me to find out about
you, but he didn't make the request for the investiga-
tive firm. I took that upon myself in order to protect his
interests.''

Danny digested that, but asked no questions. Not
many days before, the knowledge would have angered
her, but in her present frame of mind it didn't seem
particularly important. In New York she had been
living a simple life, and there wasn't much for anyone
to find out.

''If you're to understand the reasons for my action,
Mrs. Morrow, I'll have to give you some background
details. There will be no real secrets, you understand,''
Jesse added hastily, ''at least, nothing you couldn't
find out by questioning any good acquaintance of the
Whitlaw family. I would never betray confidences
about Seth's private dealings or . . . feelings.''

''Of course not,'' Danny murmured.

Jesse straightened the crease of his trousers and then
began, his facts crisply and carefully marshaled.
''Seth's mother died when the boy was very young.
After that, his father didn't remarry. He kept a succession of women—charming but not too savory, many of
them. Oh, there were a few exceptions, but for the most
part their motives were, quite simply, mercenary. As
the mistresses were installed openly in the Whitlaw
home, this wasn't always easy for Seth. When he was

nineteen, he moved out of the house. Through university, he worked for Whitcraft in the summers. You may not be aware, Mrs. Morrow, but Whitcraft was then owned by a holding company, Whitlaw Industries. It's a big, diversified corporation—prefabricated homes, lumber, various kinds of machinery, all with different company names. At that time the boats were only one of the divisions, not doing too well. Seth came up with some very revolutionary ideas for a design that would reach a larger market. He believed in the ideas. He fought for them. About fifteen years ago they were incorporated in a new boat, the Whitcraft Fisherman— you're familiar with the line, of course. It started to catch on almost at once, and it seemed that the boat division was slated to become a very profitable part of the Whitlaw operation.

"About this time, Seth's father brought home the last in the succession of his women. She was a year or two younger than Seth, a remarkably beautiful young woman, not exactly like the others.

"Mr. Whitlaw senior died of a heart attack soon after. The young woman—her name was Anne—threw herself on Seth's mercy. She cried a little and talked a lot about promises that had been made to give her a home. She didn't want jewels, she didn't want furs— and, as it happened, it could be proven that she hadn't accepted any. She claimed she had only wanted a place to live while she took a degree. And that appeared to be true too, for she was enrolled and studying at the time. I won't go through all of her hard-luck story, but the meat of it was that she seemed to be in desperate need of an opportunity to make something of herself. You may not have seen this, Mrs. Morrow, but Seth's a warm, human, sympathetic man. Because Anne was young, intelligent, not superficially jaded or grasping as some of the other women had been, he . . .

"Well, to shorten the story, in time he married her. He trusted too much, too soon, and he acted on impulse. She stung him badly. From his father, Seth had inherited fifty-one percent of Whitlaw Industries. Two cousins in the Bahamas owned the rest. Anne pretended intelligent interest in the workings of the corporation, asking questions, displaying knowledge. How she succeeded I'll never know, but somehow she wheedled Seth into presenting her with a small amount of his stock one Christmas. Need I tell you what happened? Anne and the cousins, men whom she had supposedly never even met, sold Whitlaw Industries out from under Seth for the sum of one dollar, and somehow funneled all his money back to themselves. It was done so swiftly that she was out of the country and the capital gone before it became clear what had happened. Later it was discovered that Anne and her accomplices had originally planned the con with Seth's father in mind. Let me tell you, Mrs. Morrow, it was a nasty piece of business. Seth finally regained full control of the Whitcraft division, but it took him years. It also cost him many, many millions of dollars and a great deal of hard work in the process. The rest of Whitlaw Industries will never be regained."

Jesse leaned forward to emphasize his next point. "And the worst of it was . . . I believe he actually loved his wife. Does this help you understand, if he's a little cynical about women's intentions?"

Danielle sat still, staring at her lap. She was thinking: It's true, then. Seth had not been loved for himself. And too much of his early life had been filled with women of the wrong type, so that he must have trouble distinguishing between an ordinary woman and one who used her body for advantage.

"Where women are concerned, I don't believe Seth has ever fully trusted his instincts since. Frankly, Mrs. Morrow, I haven't trusted them either. It's become a matter of course for me to check into the few amours he's been involved with over the years, always with the thought that he might someday decide to remarry. He's still a man of impulse and he's still too generous. If he became involved with another Anne . . ."

Danny looked up, her face now calm. "Thank you for telling me. It does help."

For a moment or two Jesse paid attention to the coffee cup he'd been neglecting. He was expecting questions from Danielle, and when they didn't come, he at last asked, "Aren't you wondering what I told Seth about you?"

"No. I think I already know."

"Forgive me," Jesse said penitently, "but a million dollars is a great deal of money to come up with in a few months."

When that brought only silence, he replaced the cup on his saucer and rose with a sigh to his feet. "I have to make another confession, Mrs. Morrow. I'm still not quite sure about you. I did a lot of thinking before deciding to speak to you today. I concluded there would be no harm done, either way. If you're not being wholly straightforward with Seth, then you must al-

ready know his background. And if you are being
straightforward . . . well, then, you deserve the explanation, don't you?''

Danny smiled faintly and walked him to the door.
Jesse paused on the threshold, about to go, and gave
her a curious look. ''Do you mind my asking, Mrs.
Morrow—where *did* you get that money?''

She returned his gaze levelly. Her smile had vanished. ''I won't tell, Mr. Horowitz,'' she said succinct-
ly. ''You'd only give the information to Seth. You of
all people must know the importance of being trusted
for yourself, on faith.''

When Jesse Horowitz left, he felt a little like a small
boy who had just been rapped on the knuckles. He also
had the strong, uncomfortable feeling that the Morrow
woman—even with her strained face, her smudged
work smock, and her two cents worth of long labor to
go—had the upper hand.

And Danielle had the strong, uncomfortable feeling
that the whole scene had been engineered by Seth, in an
effort to find out the truth about that million dollars.

Two weeks later Danny was reeling and numb from a
stretch of Herculean work sessions. She'd skipped all
morning swims and all sunbathing, she'd avoided the
Merriweather sisters to the point of rudeness, and
eyestrain seemed to have become a natural condition of
life. The hard work had produced three beneficial
results. It had helped dull the heaviness in her heart; it
had prevented her from mooning around the windows
of her house, hoping to catch a glimpse of Seth; and it
had disposed of all of her commissions for the summer
—all except the Watteau.

Unpleasant though it was to think of spending the rest of the summer and probably all fall on unpaid labor, it was a bitter pill that had to be swallowed unsugared.

Before starting that particular job, she decided on a trip to New York in order to deliver the finished work. The sooner delivered, the sooner she would be paid; she didn't normally demand payment in advance. She also wished to ask advice from the man under whom she'd apprenticed. The composition of older pigments varied, and she needed to research the specific paints and techniques used by Watteau. As the painting had been executed in the early years of the eighteenth century, Danny realized she would also need to procure some specialized equipment that hadn't been required for her other, ordinary jobs.

She was gone for four days—two of exhausting driving, two of research and consultation. Armed with a fresh supply of solvents, good advice, photographic equipment, some technical manuals about pigment composition, and a number of reference books about the French artist's work, she returned to Nantucket.

She imagined Seth was aware of both her departure and her return, simply because her car had been gone. She was aware of many of his movements for the same reason. She knew he went sailing often, and not only because he'd mentioned it; on occasion when his Rolls was missing, she had seen it parked in town, near the boat basin where he moored his craft.

On return to the island, she averted her head when entering her home, but she knew he was at home too. The silver Rolls was there, along with the Chevy that Jesse Horowitz used, and a small car of Japanese make.

Almost immediately, the Merriweather sisters arrived at the door for the expected visit, and although Danny was anxious to get to work, she couldn't turn them away until she'd offered tea. Nor could she deny that she hoped for some crumbs of news about Seth.

The crumbs didn't come until near the end of the visit, and they weren't very palatable.

"Well," Mildred said with a grim glint of triumph, "at least that *man* won't be bothering you again, young missie, trying to lure you into his den of iniquity." She snorted. "Him and his fancy women."

Danny's heart performed a sickening lurch, but she tried to sound unconcerned. "Oh?"

"There's only one of them, Mil," Emma reminded her sister. As always, she was readier to forgive the feebleness of the human flesh. "And she's not really so fancy." Emma smiled at Danny with her lined purse of a mouth. "She's àn actress, Danny. The same one that was here once before. She came over and talked to me the other day, when I was working in my garden."

"Oh," Danny said. The unrevealing expression was becoming a habit.

"She's in summer stock this year, working right here on Nantucket. Isn't that nice?"

"Hmmph," Mildred said. "Nothing *nice* about it. Nice is as nice does."

So that explained the extra car in Seth's drive. Danielle told herself she oughtn't to feel upset that he'd made contact with a former woman friend, but the mind was an unruly thing. She wanted to cry to the heavens at the unfairness of life and love, which forbade her living a normal existence.

Danny was glad when the sisters had gone. Heart-heavy, trying to force herself to roll up her sleeves and get back to work, she went to stand at a window overlooking the beach. It was a glorious sunny day and the sea looked inviting. With a small sense of surprise, she realized that she actually *wanted* to go for a swim, not as an exercise in conquering fear, but for simple recreation. And perhaps to work off some of her hopeless feelings about Seth.

She was considering taking time to do so, when she was given the best reason in the world not to. She saw a shapely blonde run into the surf, followed closely by Seth's big, golden, loose-limbed frame. Danny saw them splashing water at each other, and she could imagine the joyous laughter they were sharing.

Seth, for one, wasn't grieving.

She watched in silent pain until she could bear the masochism no longer, and then she turned to her work table to begin the restoration.

She photographed the painting in its frame before she began. Then, with care, she peeled away the brown-paper backing on the rear of the frame. Beneath the top layer was another layer of very old, torn backing paper, brittle with time. She photographed that too. With the eye of experience she judged that the painting had not been out of its frame since before the turn of the century. The label of an obscure New York art dealer, in Old English type, was affixed to the second layer of backing paper. After that, there were little blocks of wood and small wedges to remove, the various anchors, all of them very old, that kept the canvas and its stretcher taut in the frame. She saved the pieces meticulously, although most of them would not be reused.

At last she lifted the painting out of the frame, still on its stretcher. As always, she looked at the back of the canvas first. As she had expected, because of its age the painting had at some point been relined, probably about a century before. The humid conditions that had produced traces of mold had also loosened the paste adhesive that held the lining in sections; the layer of old glue sizing between the oils and the canvas had deteriorated for the same reason. She photographed the back to take a record of its idiosyncracies, the tiny bumps and marks that time had left on its surface.

Then she turned to the front and frowned a little. Despite the cracked paint there was the slightest flatness to the work, so that Watteau's lyric quality was not as successful as usual.

She fitted a piece of cardboard to the back, between the stretcher and the canvas, to keep the surface flat. Again she photographed the front to reveal all idiosyncracies. This time she also took photographs of the unframed canvas under raking light, from side angles, a process that would help reveal the exact irregularities of texture, the tiny bucklings and indentations, the faint striations of the brushwork, the extent of the crackle. Finally, she pulled her microscope into place to examine the canvas more closely.

When Danny lifted her head two hours later, her expression was troubled. The slight "flatness," or rather absence of depth to those colors so obscured by varnish, was not the only thing that disturbed her. She thought there was too much crackle in the areas where white had been used as an underlay. With advanced age, the pigment of flake white decayed by becoming powdery; the pigment of zinc white became brittle and cracked. Zinc white had been invented in France, but not until the end of the eighteenth century, many years after Watteau had died. It was hard to be certain of what she saw for many reasons: Not only did the dark varnish cover everything, but pigments of different kinds were always laid over each other by any artist, and that complicated the guesses.

Had the painting been retouched or overpainted at some point in its history? Considering its advanced age, that was a distinct probability, and one that might account for the slight aberrations in what she saw. She spent some additional minutes checking the canvas under ultraviolet light. No evidence of retouching appeared, but that was not conclusive; the unusually heavy layer of varnish might conceal any overpainting.

For the next two days she didn't touch the Watteau at all, except to study it in microscopic detail, and to make the tiniest of test patches along an obscure edge, trying out different solvents and confirming that some overpainting had indeed been done. Keeping a photographic record of each step, she loosened enough of the lining to examine the original canvas, in order to ascertain its age. She was also occupied in reading research on the subject and wondering if she was trying to chew more than she should have bitten off in the first place.

A lengthy long-distance phone call to New York confirmed that her fears were not totally unfounded, and reluctantly Danny concluded that she could no longer avoid speaking to Seth. If there was even the smallest possibility that his painting was a forgery, she didn't want to work on it—at least, not until the question was solved.

During the two days of fierce concentration, she had gradually become aware of one thing. The actress Seth was consorting with wasn't actually staying at East Widow. Her little car arrived about noon each day and vanished prior to theater time in the early evening. To be aware of the comings and goings, Danny hardly had to look out the window. The sound of a car, on this back road, was rare.

That didn't mean that Mildred's worst expectations weren't being realized, of course. Danny decided it would be safest to see Seth by appointment, at a prearranged time.

"There's no use putting it off," she scolded herself as she picked up the phone. It was morning, and she hoped the hour might be convenient.

When Jesse Horowitz answered, Danny identified herself. She would have made the arrangements with him, but before she could do so Seth came on the line.

"Well?" he asked. His voice was chilled.

"I want to come and speak to you about your painting, Seth."

"I've been wondering how long it would take you to cry uncle. How far along are you?"

"I haven't started yet."

"Well, well. So . . . the incorruptible Mrs. Morrow does have a hard head for a dollar, after all. I suppose you'll be giving me a revised quote?"

His sarcasm hurt, but Danny held her temper. "May I come over right now?"

Seth's small silence suggested that he was thinking. "No. I'll come over there in a few minutes. I'll meet you on your terrace. With the Merriweather binoculars to keep the peace," he added in a bitterly mocking tone, "it's the most neutral territory I can think of, short of the beach."

"Fine," Danny agreed. It wasn't to be a social visit, so she changed no clothes, prepared no coffee or lemonade. She watched through the study doors until she saw Seth coming over from his own house. He moved slowly—unwillingly, she thought—with a tread heavier than his usual lithe male grace. She remembered the warm golden aura that had seemed to surround him the first time she'd seen him, and realized that a great part of his vitality was lacking.

She slipped through the doors, closing them but leaving them unlocked, in case she wanted access to the canvas or any of the research that supported her theory.

Seth refused an invitation to take a chair, so Danny stood too. His distant manner caused her throat to hurt, but at least it made it easier for her to remain business-like herself.

There was no particular need for preamble, so she expressed her doubts at once, going over each small detail that had troubled her. "The first thing that bothered me was just . . . well, intuition. If it's a Watteau, it's not quite up to his usual work, because it lacks something. Then there's the way it's crackled. I think there may be zinc white here and there on that painting, and there shouldn't be." She explained about the date of its invention.

"Superficially, the back of the canvas appeared about the right age, but on closer inspection, I had a hunch it wasn't. It didn't *feel* quite right to my eyes. It would take laboratory analysis to determine more about the age of the fibers. With my equipment I certainly couldn't be sure, but these things were enough to start me wondering."

There were other questionable factors: minuscule details of composition and brushstroke, usually as personal as an artist's signature. Again, it might take sophisticated equipment to determine the truth, possibly X-ray equipment and more powerful magnification than Danny's microscope was capable of.

"If it's a forgery, it's a good one, barring the use of the wrong pigment. None of this is conclusive, of course, because in matters like this I'm no more than an educated amateur—you need a Watteau expert. But I do think there's a chance the painting isn't authentic. The final clue, and it's an important one, is the name of the dealer who sold this to some member of your family, back before the turn of the century. According to my adviser in New York, the man did sell a number of good forgeries that were uncovered years later."

To avoid eye contact with Seth, Danielle had been looking into the distance, at the sea. Now, with her revelations complete, she turned toward him and surprised his eyes on her. Her breath caught in her throat and her heart started to beat faster at the expression on his face. It was the expression of a man in pain, and she knew in that moment that he had not stopped wanting her. .

He looked as though he had not heard a word she'd said, only the sound of her voice.

With effort, he shook himself out of his obsessive reverie. "What are you recommending?" he asked. He didn't sound surprised, only depressed.

Danny jammed her hands into the pockets of her

smock. She had become very conscious of all things about her person—her tired face, her burned-out eyes, the weight she'd lost, the crumpled work clothes that smelled of chemicals. "You should have the painting authenticated before any work is done on it. I wouldn't want to recommend the right expert. The Boston Museum of Fine Arts could advise you."

"Fine." But Seth sounded as though he didn't much care.

"It's out of the frame now, but I'll get it together as soon as possible. Then you can have it back. I'll bring it over tomorrow."

"Jesse will pick it up from you on the weekend. He's off to Boston on Monday morning and he'll be there all week, supervising some small renovations being done at my house. He can look into it then."

There was very little more to say. Danny added quietly, "I'm sorry, Seth."

He opened his mouth almost as if to say something. Then, without expressing whatever was on his mind, he slowly turned away and walked back to East Widow. His retreating figure looked . . . defeated.

Danny felt defeated too. For the first time in days she didn't have to race back to work. She had nothing, absolutely nothing, to do. Exhausted, she should have welcomed the lack of occupation, but the emptiness of the hours ahead only served to remind her of the great emptiness in her life. She slumped down on a lounge chair and tried to let the heat of the healing sun reach her. After a few minutes she tiredly peeled off her work smock to uncover the lighter T-shirt beneath.

And then she stretched out on the lounge chair and

laid the work smock over her face, because she was too
damn tired to walk back into the house and find a pair
of sunglasses.

Empty, empty, empty . . . tired, tired, tired . . .

She woke groggily, to Emma Merriweather shaking
her arm. Disoriented at first, Danny didn't know how
long she'd been asleep. Her dazed eyes came open to
see the familiar snowy hair and wrinkled face bending
over her. Emma looked very upset.

"Danny, Danny . . . oh, dear, oh, dear," she was
saying in a quaking, quivering voice. "You must wake
up. Oh, *dear*."

Alarm spiked Danny into alertness. She sat bolt
upright. "What's the matter, Emma? Is something
wrong? Is it . . . Mildred?"

"No, no . . . but you must come. Oh, dear!"

There was something different about Emma, and it
took Danny a moment to realize that the steel-rimmed
spectacles were missing from the bridge of her nose.
Behind her, the door into the study was wide open; she
had come through the house that way.

"I've done something awful . . . oh, dear . . . I
can't be sure *what* I've done . . . you must come and
see, Danny . . . I was bringing you some tea, I wanted
to talk to you, and you looked so worn out . . . and
then I dropped the tray, and now . . . oh, dear . . . I
made a terrible mess . . . I think I've broken my
glasses too . . . they fell, you see, when I bent over to
mop the floor . . . and I think I heard them crack,
Danny . . . but I can't see to find them . . . I tried to
clean everything up, but . . ."

Danny soothed Emma's flutterings enough to discover that the scene of disaster, whatever it was, was in her own study. Pierced with anxiety, still trying to reassure Emma, she hurried through the doors into her house. The strong smell of solvent immediately assailed her nostrils.

"It all started this morning, when I couldn't find my lucky bent penny . . . oh, dear, I *knew* this would be a bad day . . . I've done everything wrong . . . I would have asked Mildred to help, but I knew she'd be angry with me . . . she didn't even want me to come over and tell you . . . and I spilled salt this morning too . . . oh, goodness, what a day. Can you see my glasses anywhere, Danny?"

It wasn't easy, in the scene of minor carnage that confronted Danielle. On the work table there was a tangle of broken teacups, teabags, upended bottles of chemicals, and over everything the ooze of spilled liquid. Several bunched tea towels, brown with the stain of tannic acid, testified to Emma's ineffectual efforts to mop up. Larger terry towels, on the floor surrounding the desk, had been laid down to soak up the spills that still dripped slowly here and there.

"I hope I got the towels down in time to save the floor," Emma said worriedly.

She admitted that she had spent half an hour trying to repair the damage, but in the hunt for her glasses, things had gone from bad to worse. "I broke one of your bottles too, Danny. I could tell by the smell. I was going to wipe it up at once, but it was just like acid, it burned my fingers. I had to stop and wash my hands. Then I got a bigger towel so I wouldn't touch it again. Oh, dear . . ."

"Are your hands all right?"

"Oh, yes. I just touched a teeny drop. Oh, dear, oh *dear*."

The spectacles, Danny saw, had fallen close to the desk. They weren't broken. She bent and picked them up and handed them to Emma, but her mind was really on the crumpled, discolored terry bath towel lying on top of the one canvas on the work surface. It had been stained like the others, but the stains were not all tea.

She lifted the towel, saw what Emma had done, felt her stomach freeze. Her logical brain took over. Hastily but gently, she covered the painting with a different towel, one that still retained some absorbency. The best thing she could do at this point was get Emma out of here.

"Is it all right?" Emma asked anxiously.

Danny started to steer her to the door. "Yes, of course, Emma. Now run along. You've cleaned up the worst, and I'd rather do the rest alone. You go home and look for your lucky penny. We'll have tea tomorrow, when it's safer for you to be out and about."

"At first I didn't see that picture in the mess. I'm glad it's not a really *big* painting, Danny, like the Sargent. I dried it all up, but I couldn't see too well . . . Will it be all right?"

"Absolutely."

Emma resisted the gentle push toward the door. "I have to help you clean up, Danny, and then I have to talk to you. It's very important. There's something I—"

Danny was firm. "Hurry home, Emma, or Mildred might walk in on this mess. We'll have tea tomorrow, *after* you've found your lucky penny."

It was indeed Emma's unlucky day, and Danny's

too. Out of its frame, with the canvas absorbing moisture through back as well as front, Seth's painting had been thoroughly inundated with damaging substances. Tea had attacked the canvas from the rear, and the moisture, worst enemy of old glue sizing, had loosened some of the paint from the canvas. What tea had not accomplished, solvent had. The broken bottle, Danny soon determined, had contained dimethyl formamide, which she had been using in one of her tiny test patches to remove a few flakes of stubborn overpainting. It was the strongest, trickiest and most dangerous of her various potions, one she would never dream of using indiscriminately.

Emma's unskilled efforts to scrub the surface of the canvas dry had accomplished everything the solvent had started. The Watteau, if it had been a Watteau, was hardly more than a damp piece of old canvas covered with smears. In places the oil still clung, leaving the painting recognizable; but to all effects and purposes it was ruined. Nothing would reverse the damage.

The ice in Danny's stomach was fortunately matched by the ice in her head. It had become a matter of personal urgency to find out if the painting was—had been—a forgery. She picked up the phone and called New York. Thank God for her museum and art gallery contacts, which should facilitate everything.

Again, ill luck seemed to be the order of the day. The man who had trained her in her trade was not available. Danny then remembered that a few days before, when she'd been in New York, he'd told her he was going on holiday.

After several calls she managed to connect with the owner of a small, reputable gallery that specialized in

eighteenth- and nineteenth-century European paintings. Authenticating was one of his specialties, and
Danny had had some dealings with him in the past.

She explained the sequence of events and the urgency of her quest, and extracted from him a promise to
have the canvas and the composition of paints analyzed
immediately. On the inches where the painting was
relatively intact, the brushstrokes and style could also
be examined. In addition, Danny had the crumbling
brown paper backing with the dealer's imprint on it, a
further clue to the history of the work. And she had all
the photographs showing every tiny idiosyncracy of the
original.

"I'll bundle up the whole mess and bring it to New
York at once," she said.

"Weekend coming up," the man reminded her.

"Monday, then," Danny said, cursing the five-day
work week.

She could do no more for the moment. She hung up.
Her mind still worked clearly. Thank God she'd
warned Seth that the Watteau might be a forgery.

She realized she'd have to tell him what had happened. It would mean another confrontation, possibly
an unpleasant one, but one that couldn't be avoided.
Danny knew she would have to face up to the task
before Jesse Horowitz arrived at her door to collect the
painting.

She looked at her wristwatch and realized with dull
surprise that her nap on the patio must have been a
lengthy one, three or four hours. She'd slept through
lunch and half the afternoon, and the hands on the
watch were not the only testament. Since waking,
she'd been too caught up in serious matters to notice

that her arms had become very red. Danny's ivory-gold skin didn't always sunburn so easily, but this year she hadn't spent enough time outdoors to build up a good foundation of tan.

Her legs had been protected by jeans and her face by the covering of the smock, but her arms were badly sunburned. In fact, they hurt like hell. She touched one and gasped, realizing that the worst of the burn probably had yet to appear. It was only the last of a lot of straws, and Danny buried her face in her hands while shakiness took over from calm control.

When the tremors lessened and her brain started to function again, she made her way to a window from which she could see the driveway of East Widow. As the little Japanese car was there, she realized that this was not a good time to approach Seth. She'd have to wait till later, when the actress left for her evening performance.

Slowly Danny walked back into her study to clean up the rest of the disaster area.

The faint echo of laughter reached her ears through the open doors. She walked over to shut them and caught a glimpse of two swimmers lying in the sun down by the beach, in full view of Middle Widow. From here, it looked as though Seth's friend had pillowed her pretty head on his stomach. A sudden rage stabbed Danielle. How dare he have a good time while she was having a rotten one?

She realized that along with everything else, she had become very, very angry with Seth Whitlaw. It wasn't Emma who'd created this godawful mess—it was *him*.

Chapter Ten

*W*hen the doorbell rang, Seth was sprawled on his bed with his fingers laced behind his head, staring unseeingly at the ceiling. He had been lying that way for nearly an hour, brooding into nothingness ever since his afternoon's companion had departed. Now night had closed in outside, and there was nothing to distract him from the leaden heaviness in his chest.

Every nerve ending in his body turned raw at the sound of the door—a reaction that had become commonplace every time anyone arrived at East Widow nowadays—but he didn't stir. His jaw tensed, though, and his ears became finely attuned to the small sounds and murmurs that accompanied the answering of the door.

"She's here again," Jesse Horowitz said when he appeared at the bedroom door. He didn't say who "she" was. Seth already knew, anyway. He had reacted like a Geiger counter to the muffled rise and fall of her husky voice, even though the words had not been intelligible.

Seth moved no more than the muscles required to speak. "What does she want?"

"She said it was business."

"What mood?"

"With her, it's hard to tell, Seth."

"Clothes?"

"Nothing special. Cotton shirt, cotton skirt, very plain. Not like the last time. She looks very tired."

Seth shifted restlessly to lay a hand loosely over his eyes. "You deal with her, Jesse. I'm damned if I want to. That exhausted act gets to me—Anne used to use it too, along with the rest of her bag of tricks. If the Morrow woman keeps it up, one of these days I'm going to—"

Oh, no, you're not, Seth Whitlaw, he reminded himself grimly. You are *not* going to propose. You held your tongue earlier in the day, and you can bloody well hold it tonight, if you have to bite it off.

". . . shake her till she rattles," he finished through his teeth, at last levering himself upright. His long legs were still clad in the white ducks he'd worn for a late-afternoon sail with his actress acquaintance, and a white velour sweatshirt molded his upper torso.

"I did try to find out what she wants, Seth, but she won't talk to me. She said she had to speak to you. And she said it was very, very urgent."

Seth's low curse was explicit and unpleasant, but it was accompanied by a flinging of his legs over the side of the bed. He took time only to lace his feet into the white suede boat shoes he'd removed earlier.

"Don't bother bringing drinks to the living room. But put a brandy bottle beside my bed, will you, Jesse? I have a feeling I'm going to be needing it."

"Seth, last time—"

"Stow it, Jesse! A man doesn't need lectures when a woman's about to get the better of him."

On the verge of leaving the room, he wheeled for a last word with his man. "On second thought," he said glumly, "make it a bottle of champagne, just in case."

"Two glasses?"

Seth glowered. "Do you have to be told? And stop looking at me like that, dammit. There's no need to outguess me just because I'm having a few renovations done at the house. If I do lose my head and ask, there is not one single . . . sweet . . . reason to celebrate."

Jesse hid a smile in his beard. After his last visit next door, about three weeks earlier, he had decided that Danielle Morrow would do his employer very, very well indeed. Her proud refusal to reveal the secret of where she'd acquired money had carried conviction. Jesse had reasoned that if her motives were less than pure, she would have had easy explanations at the ready. He had reported everything to his employer, as requested, but Seth had not been similarly convinced.

"My God, Jesse!" Seth had exploded at the time. "Can't you remember the way my sainted wife used to operate? If nothing else convinced me about Danielle Morrow, that trick with the emerald pin did. Anne would have done exactly the same thing. And one con woman in a lifetime is more than enough for me."

Seth, descending the stairs, was remembering the same scene, and trying to hang on to his senses by reminding himself of the various ways he'd been softened up years before. The innocent eyes . . . the pretense of noble motives . . . the simple logic of everything Anne did or said. During the two years of his marriage he had been deeply in love. And yet, all the while, Anne had been playing him for a fool, twisting him around her finger again and again, until he trusted her implicitly, until he became as pliant as knitting yarn in her hands. And that had been the worst hell of it: giving his heart and his trust to a woman who'd had no feelings at all for him. The game she had played was one she'd started long before they had even met. She'd bilked other men before him, and he supposed she'd bilked other men since.

He came to a halt in the door of the living room. Danny was on her feet too. She was standing near the fireplace, slender and outwardly composed, with a floor lamp nearby burnishing the rich fire-lights in her hair. She was dressed in serene gray-green, a soft, subtle color like moss in a shady forest.

She was so . . . still, so beautiful, Seth thought, that she might have been a portrait. The man in him fought with the cynic, and the man almost won.

The magnetism between them kept both silent for a time. Danny felt pulled by it, unwilling to break the quiet by an immediate revelation of her bad news, as she had intended. It was not entirely a physical pull. Seth's bronzed attractiveness was heightened by the whites he wore, but Danielle was too darn tired to react fully to physical attraction. The yearning she felt was quite different. She wanted to cross the room and walk into his arms, and simply rest her head against his shoulder for a while and have him hold her close, and then maybe pummel his chest angrily for a few minutes to work out some of her frustrated feelings, and finally have a good cry against the same broad expanse.

Instead of crossing the room, she crossed her arms and rubbed her fingers gently and gingerly against the blisters of a flaming sunburn, now hidden by long sleeves. The pain helped to inject her with pride, reminding her of the day's happenings.

Seth walked into the room slowly, without saying a word, and for a few moments Danny had the impression that the pull he felt was not so very different from her own.

She started talking before he reached her, because she didn't want to break down and weep until she had told him the full story. Seth came to a halt a few feet away and listened without comment.

Quietly and quickly, Danny gave him a simplified version of the accident in her study, only leaving out Emma Merriweather's part in it. She didn't wish to blame an old lady of eighty-five who wasn't even aware of the damage she had done. And Danny knew the fault was partially her own, first for not locking the study doors, then for falling asleep so deeply that she hadn't even heard the sound of a dropping tray.

She had finished the whole tale, including her intention of taking the ruined canvas to New York for analysis, and still Seth hadn't spoken. His eyes remained fastened on her mouth, as if he expected her to say more. His face was a mask, and she couldn't tell what he was thinking.

When he did speak, at first she could not believe her ears. His voice was slow, cruel, and cynical, with a cynicism born of old, bad experience. And his eyes—

they were like lasers, cutting into her with anger and hurtful contempt.

"Very clever indeed. And exactly when did you replace my canvas with a suitable one? You've had three weeks to work out the details, Danielle, and I'm sure you've worked them out very well indeed. In your line of work, it shouldn't be hard to acquire a canvas of the right size and approximate age. When did you do that—during your last trip to New York?"

"Seth," she whispered, and it felt as if her heart had turned white. Certainly, her face had been drained of color.

He jammed his hands into his pockets, as though only by doing this could he restrain himself from attacking her with means more physical than words. "Congratulations, Mrs. Morrow. I can see your plan now, in all its beautiful simplicity. First you warn me that my painting might be a forgery, just in case later lab analysis proves that your substitution couldn't possibly have been a Watteau. Then you ruin it—who can tell what picture lies beneath a mass of smears? Or perhaps you expect I won't even pursue the question of forgery, because it would be easier for me to collect the insurance if I didn't. Have you found a market for the *real* canvas yet? What's the going rate in the underground art market? Three hundred thousand . . . or less . . . or *more?*"

Danny's face felt as if it would crack if she tried to talk. She stood like a statue, too shocked to defend herself, too benumbed to even consider whether there were holes in Seth's logic. All the feeling seemed to have left her body.

"Diabolical, and so much safer than an outright theft. My God! Is *that* how you made your million some years ago? By working a similar scam? Well, no wonder you can't do it too often! You have to wait for the right painting . . . the right circumstances . . . the right mark. Well, dammit, I'm not the right mark. Don't bother taking the canvas to New York at all, Danielle, because the only thing you'll prove is exactly what you want to prove. And I'm not buying that."

When feeling returned to Danielle, it returned with a vengeance. The little tremors started in her legs. They traveled up through her limbs, grew in intensity as they rose to the inside of her stomach, turned to churning nausea, reached her chest with the force of a burning acid. Her chest heaved, and she knew she must leave or make a fool of herself. Blindly, with poker-stiff shoulders and head held high, she started to walk toward the door.

As she passed him, Seth seized her upper arms. His fingers dug in mercilessly, and pride couldn't prevent the cry of pain as he gripped her blistered arms.

His voice had turned to an intense hiss. "I'll give you exactly one week to produce one of two things— my painting, the *genuine* one in the same condition, or the money you made from selling it."

She had clamped her mouth over the first involuntary gasp of pain. She could taste the blood where her teeth bit into her bottom lip. *And what if I can't produce?* she wanted to cry. *What then?*

But the words could not be said. She had to get out immediately or face a total loss of pride, for she had no doubt that she was going to be physically ill.

She tore herself away. The blistery surface of her

skin tore away too, but by then she didn't even feel it. She was racing through the door . . . running through the night, holding her mouth, with hair streaming wildly . . . and she didn't even know the direction she had taken until she found herself at the shore.

No moon silvered the waves on that clouded night, and darkness mercifully cloaked her ignominy. Danny kneeled in several inches of water and retched and retched and retched again, where rising tide and lapping waves would soon wash away all secrets.

She hated him. She hated him. She *hated* him.

When she finally rose to her feet, she was outwardly calm again, drained of the worst of the poison inside her. But the eyes that turned toward the lighted windows of East Widow were filled with something new and cold and hard, an acid as corrosive as that she had just voided.

In that dark night, with soaked legs and blistered arms and a heart filled with a great hatred, she promised herself that Seth Whitlaw would never again have the capacity to hurt her.

Chapter Eleven

*W*hat would *you* do, Danielle?'' Danny whispered.

The portrait stood in silence, cloaked in pride, the quiet green eyes looking eternally out to sea.

Danny was standing too, facing her alter ego, asking for solutions she couldn't find herself. Her face, as she searched the face of the other Danielle, mirrored none of the sadness reflected in that of her ancestor. Her eyes held only the signs of a restless night and the cold hard light of determination.

Pride was a difficult thing, and Danny had the Fielding pride. With a fierceness that consumed her, she wanted to demonstrate to Seth, in some forceful and incontrovertible way, that he was dead wrong about her. She would, too; but she wouldn't lower her dignity to do it.

There were fallacies in his reasoning, but she was too stung by his accusations to point them out. Nine years before, at the time when he believed her to have executed some million-dollar coup in art theft, she'd had access to no important paintings at all. She had simply been an underling, hired for miscellaneous jobs in the bowels of a large museum. Apprenticing to a conservator had come a little later in time.

Moreover, the odds against finding a "twin" canvas in a matter of three short weeks were so enormous that they were almost beyond the realm of possibility. But how could Seth be expected to know that?

Enough of the purported Watteau remained intact to show that no canvas could have been substituted. Even with his untutored eye, after a cursory inspection of the ruined work, Seth would probably have to concede that he was wrong. *Probably.* Under the circumstances, that was a big word. An expert would most certainly know on sight, especially with the photographs that showed every tiny idiosyncracy of the canvas's original state both back and front. But Seth wasn't an expert. And Danny refused to go through the exercise of trying to convince him of anything at all.

She could have told where she'd made the money years before. She knew why Jesse Horowitz's investigations hadn't turned up evidence of her stock transactions: she hadn't done them in her own name. At that point in time, the name of Morrow had been anathema on Wall Street, particularly in the firm where Roger had been employed. Clive Hamilton, the senior partner through whom she'd worked, had traded for her in his own name, using her stake from the sale of East Widow and following her instructions. She had no proof of this, but Clive would attest to it if she asked. After Danny had stopped trading, when her strung-out nerves had finally caught up with her and told her that her luck was sure to run out, Clive had continued to wine and dine her in a series of lunches, trying to get market tips. He hadn't believed that she could parlay so little money into so much, in so short a time, without inside information. Disgustedly, Danny reminded herself that Seth would probably assume she'd had inside information too, acquired in some devious way.

She could have called on Emma Merriweather to recount the exact circumstances of the accident, although that would mean causing a great deal of distress to an old lady who was already very upset by her clumsiness. Danny wouldn't do it.

She wanted Seth to eat humble pie, but by this point she refused to eat a single bite herself. One more disbelieving look from him, and her pride would stick in her craw. He'd mistrusted her once too often, insulted her once too often, hurt her once too often. She scorned uttering the protests of a weakling, for even if he was eventually forced to admit his error, she would have felt cheapened to demean herself with the effort of convincing him.

"I'd rather stand on Main Street and undress myself," she told her alter ego. "And if it proved anything, believe me, I *would*."

She supposed she could simply give Seth's ruined painting back at the end of a week and let him make what he would of it. In time, some art expert would support her—if he bothered to take it to one. At the moment it was the only recourse she could think of.

"Or is it the only way . . . ?" she asked herself, with her eyes hardening suddenly. They fastened on the portrait with new purpose. "Is it . . . ? Yes, I'll do it. This time I'll do it. You *are* going to solve everything for me after all, Danielle Fielding."

The solution took shape in her brain quickly, and although it was not a solution she liked, it was one that answered pride. Selling the valuable work of art on such short notice wouldn't be easy, though. Auctions took weeks, sometimes months; galleries worked on commission and wouldn't sell in a rush; and private collectors, even if she knew any rich enough to afford the work, would be cautious and move slowly while confirming the painting's worth.

She needed an instant buyer who could come up with the money to buy, someone who would take the plunge without stalling, someone who would deal with her purely on trust.

Someone like Clive Hamilton.

Clive. Of course! He didn't know a thing about art, but he didn't have to. He was a speculator. If he had a chance of doubling an investment in a matter of months, or maybe doing even better than that, he would have to listen. He also trusted her implicitly. As he was associated with the same firm where Roger had worked, he was well aware that she had settled all the differences arising from Roger's misguided stock transactions. In matter of fact, contrary to Jesse Horowitz's assumption, Danny had not been legally obligated to do any such thing. A court of law could have seized Roger's nonexistent estate, but not her father's, not the houses or the long, valuable stretch of shoreline incorporating the Three Widows.

Clive knew these things, and he knew that the

money she'd restored would otherwise have had to come from his own pocket and the pockets of his partners, if the firm was to maintain its good solid reputation on Wall Street. What Danielle had done from self-respect, to prevent her dead husband's dishonor, had saved Clive Hamilton a considerable amount of money.

Reaching him would likely be as easy as dialing the phone, because he ought to be at his office. It was Friday, not a holiday, and the New York exchange was open.

He came on the line at once. "Clive? This is Danielle Morrow. A voice out of the past."

"Danny! Well, for goodness' sake. Just the sort of surprise I needed on a gray day like today. What about lunch?" Clive's interest long ago had not been purely professional.

"I'm calling from Nantucket, Clive. This is strictly a business call."

"Well, well. I thought you'd sworn off the Dow Jones. About to take another headlong dive? Make yourself a killing?"

"No, Clive, but *you're* about to—if you can come up with three hundred thousand dollars by next week."

"That's talking big money. I'd have to sell some of my portfolio, and I'm not sure I . . . well . . . go on, Danny. I'm listening."

"I can't absolutely promise that you'll double it in a matter of months, but . . ."

Clive listened attentively. The Sargent had been evaluated for insurance purposes at seven hundred thousand dollars, and it would probably bring a rock-bottom minimum of six at auction. It might do a lot better.

When she hung up, Danny had her buyer.

The triumph was short-lived, for the eyes of the portrait came back to haunt her. She went to look at them again, this time with regret becoming large in her heart. A deal was a deal, and she wouldn't renege; but she knew she would not be glad when Clive arrived in Nantucket, as he had promised to do early the following week, in order to view his unseen purchase and deliver a check. Seth would have his money within days.

"At first," Danny whispered to her namesake, "he thought I wanted to sell myself. And now I have. Oh, God, I have—or at least it feels like it. I'm sorry, Danielle."

She'd forgotten about Emma. For once, perhaps in repentance for the previous day's happenings, Emma didn't walk right in. She rang the doorbell, and her creased old face wore a very tentative expression, as if she half expected the whole house to collapse simply because of her presence.

"I haven't found my lucky penny yet," she sighed as she stepped cautiously inside. "Everything's been going wrong, Danny. You can't imagine. I found aphids in my rosebushes, I got a run in my stocking, and this morning the mailman didn't bring a single thing but circulars. It's not just bad things coming in threes, either. I had another terrible argument with Mildred, too. And now it looks as though it might rain."

Danny laughed half-heartedly, because the various crises sounded as if they were all in a normal day. "Relax, Emma. I found your bent penny on the floor in my study, when I was cleaning up. It must have fallen out of your pocket when you were looking for your glasses. Perhaps you'd forgotten where it was. I would have brought it over but . . . I've had other-things on my mind."

Emma was enormously relieved. With the bent penny restored to her, she sat down at Danny's large old kitchen table and chattered about small nothings while the kettle came to a boil.

"But none of that is what I *really* came to say," she admitted worriedly once Danny had taken a chair facing her. The kitchen table was a comfortable, familiar place to sit, with elbows on the table and old memories to share.

"Yesterday I was going through some things in the attic," Emma started. "I found a box of old Fielding letters, and I was going to bring them to you. Mildred said I mustn't. We had a fight, Danny. I told her the letters were *yours,* and she said yes, but she didn't want you to see them, at least not yet. She took the box away from me and locked it up."

Behind the spectacles, Emma's rheumy old eyes began to fill. "It was a bad fight, Danny. I cried. Mil got upset too. She wasn't too careful with her tongue, and I learned a lot of things she'd been hiding from me, and from you too. She says you shouldn't be told the truth until there's some God-fearing man courting you, maybe a nice widower with honorable intentions, someone who knows how to keep his hands to himself until he's properly churched. She says you're too modern. She says you might . . . well, I hate to say it, the expression Mil used . . . she said you might *lift your skirts* again, like you did for Roger Morrow. Now I know it wasn't like that at all, Danny. But that's what Mil said you might do, if you knew.''

"If I knew what?'' Danny asked, her voice deathly quiet.

"The real story,'' Emma said in her cobwebby voice, sounding very upset. "Mil's known it for years, but she didn't tell me until I'd read a thing or two in that box. She didn't trust me not to tell you. It's all to do with those words on the portrait, Danny. They're not true. And I can prove it.''

"Not true,'' Danny whispered. All those years, all those fears . . . wasted, all wasted. . . .

She struggled to put her logical mind in order. There was more to find out. If Emma, custodian of family superstition, had been convinced, the truth must be very convincing indeed. And Emma held the key to everything in her head.

Urgently Danny asked, "Tell me, Emma. Just start at the beginning. What's the first thing?''

"First I'll tell about Jethro Fielding. He didn't die at sea, he died in Tahiti, where his ship stopped to fill the watercasks on the way back from China. He was torn asunder all right, but it was alcohol that did it. When all his men were ashore with those girls in grass skirts, he started drinking because . . . well, I suppose he was real lonely for his wife, Danny. He'd been at sea for months and months, but he didn't want to be unfaithful to her. When his first bottle ran out, he . . . well, he

wasn't thinking straight by then. He opened his mouth
and poured most of a second bottle right down his
throat, without stopping. He died of alcohol poisoning.
The big wave was just to hush things up. You see, it
wasn't considered respectable for him to be tippling
like that. Only two people knew the truth, the first mate
and the ship's doctor. It was the ship's doctor who told
Danielle Fielding."

Danny stared. "How on earth would you know that?
It couldn't have been in a letter."

"Mil told me. And she found out from . . . but I'll
get to that in time. Now don't confuse me, Danny. I'm
an old lady and if I tell things out of order, I might
forget something." Emma wiped her glasses and took a
steadying breath. "Those dreadful brothers-in-law, the
ones that were ogling Danielle Fielding, well . . . once
she was a widow, they tried to take advantage of her.
They told her they'd spread nasty scandal about her if
she didn't . . . well, you know . . ."

Danny sat in silence, trying to put herself into the
mind of a woman who had died nearly a century
before. With no trouble, because she had done it so
often in the past, she succeeded. She whispered,
almost to herself, "And so she created a scandal
herself, just to show them she didn't care." And
perhaps to warn their wives that they'd better keep
their eyes open. "But . . ."

Emma had conquered her tearfulness and remembered the happy parts of the news she was imparting.
Her face had started to glow. "There's more, Danny.
Danielle Fielding didn't die at sea either. She got all the
way back to France. She lived to a ripe age, too. There

were letters from her in the box, written to her daughter, and one of them was dated 1919. She was seventy then. That was when her daughter died, so of course it was the last letter. It sounded as though she was managing her father's estates in Normandy. She wrote a little bit about how glad she was that her daughter was helping the suffragettes, and how it looked like they were going to win in the States, and how she thought she might start fighting for the women's vote in France. She said she wanted to vote just once before she died.''

"But the words on the painting . . .''

"Mr. Sargent didn't put them on at all. They were painted on years later, Danny. Mil heard that right from the mouth of someone who saw them being painted.''

For a moment Emma looked as though she was going to burst with the importance of what she had to say. "It was Danielle herself who did it. She did it on account of her daughter.''

"The suffragette?''

"Yes. Though she wasn't a suffragette when the words were put on. She was only a young girl then, just turned seventeen. Danielle Fielding had to go back to France to see her father, because he was dying of some slow disease, consumption I think. But she didn't like to leave her daughter, especially as she knew she might be in France for a long time. Already, there were a lot of suitors mooning around Middle Widow. The girl said she could look out for herself, even though her older brother was off to sea by then, and her father of course was dead. Well, Danielle thought her daughter could handle most of the men around, except for one who'd been trying a thing or two on the sly." Emma lowered her voice; there were some sins she did find shocking. "It was the girl's own uncle, the man in West Widow. Yes, Danny, one of the very same men—the other was dead by then. No one could send him packing because, by Jethro's will, he was actually the girl's legal guardian.

"So before she left for France, Danielle painted those lines, and invented some of the story, and had the portrait brought downstairs from her bedroom. She let things slip and the servants gossiped, and soon the rumors spread about how two men had died just from touching her. She murmured her fears about how the curse might affect her daughter, who looked so much like her and had the same name. Oh, that Danielle Fielding, she thought of everything. She said she was afraid the curse might even kill *her*. Later, after she had left for France, the daughter spread news that it had. Well, *three* people dead proved it was a curse that no one could ignore. And the trick worked, too. That dreadful man never touched his niece again."

"You certainly didn't learn all that from an old letter!"

"No. Mil was told it, by someone who ought to know. When we were arguing, it all came out. And the person who told Mil everything was . . ." Emma paused triumphantly, "that first Danielle's daughter."

She waited until Danny had digested that, and then rambled on. "Mil used to admire her, you see. When Mildred was young, just a girl in this house, she used to think she would become a suffragette herself. Once, she swore she wouldn't marry until women got the vote." Emma sighed and shook her head. "I used to wonder why all that changed, but the other day I found out. When we were fighting, Mil let it slip that Danielle's daughter had lived common law with a man. When Mil found that out, she decided she'd better not associate herself with such goings-on."

Emma's face brightened. "So you see, Danny, that curse doesn't mean a thing, for it didn't kill a soul. No one died at sea except those nasty men, and they didn't touch Danielle Fielding at all." Emma sighed, a rueful, rusty sound. "Mildred used to say it was sinful to fill you with superstitious twaddle, and I suppose this time she was right."

"But you didn't know the truth," Danny said thoughtfully. She was wondering which of the two old sisters had been the real sinner.

"And I suppose you mean, Mildred did. Well, that's so. But don't be too mad at her, Danny. She loves you. Yesterday she said it was a tiny white sin to stop a big, black one that might send you right into the devil's arms. And she didn't lie, she only listened to *me* lie. She said she was just trying to keep you out of trouble when you were young . . . and, well, it's true, some teenagers *do* carry on these days. She thought the story would make you behave yourself."

"It did," Danny admitted. But she wasn't thinking of when she had been in her teens.

After Emma had gone, Danny made her way to the study. First—admittedly prompted by mild superstition —she took a weighty reference book off the shelf. In the encyclopedia she found what she wanted listed under Women's Suffrage. In France it had come in

1945, when Danielle Fielding would have been ninety-six years old.

"And I bet you voted, too," Danny said, directing her words to her silent ancestress. She felt a good deal of pride along with the tiny prick of tears. For a musing moment she wondered if the other Danielle had lived through World War II . . . if, at that advanced age, she had provided shelter for escaped airmen . . . if she had helped the Resistance . . . if she had sometimes tricked the Nazis too, just as she had tricked a man into leaving her daughter alone. . . .

But that was only wishful thinking, born of Danny's pride in her ancestry. The whole story of that first Danielle Fielding would never be known. It didn't matter. "I think you were an extraordinary woman," Danny murmured. "I wish I were just like you."

After she had paid her homage, Danny directed a bright light at the lower part of the Sargent. She kneeled and looked at the faint lettering on the portrait, first by eye and then with her magnifying headset. She had never looked so closely before. She realized that the words didn't have the gloss of the varnish around them. They had also been made deliberately faint, she guessed, to obscure the flaws of letters less perfect than an artist's hand would have made—and perhaps also to fool the eyes of people who might have seen the portrait in passing before the legend was painted on.

Normally Danny would touch no painting except in a horizontal position. But she would be removing very little from the surface, and none of the varnish at all. After a moment or two of indecision, she set to work. The painting had been sold, and the old tampering ought to be removed before it was delivered.

> *Whoso takes this woman in love*
> *The sea shall tear asunder*

The legend was in tempera paint, and it came off with no trouble. Mineral spirits, which had no solvent effect on varnish, wiped the words away with no harm to the painting beneath. In a gentle rolling motion of Danny's swab, they were gone. A dry swab immediately followed the dampened one, leaving the canvas intact.

> *Untouched, untouchable let her be*
> *Or lie ten fathom under*

And in a few more minutes it was as though the words had never been.

Danny looked at the cotton swab in her hand, discolored with all that remained of Danielle Fielding's handiwork. This was all that was left of a childhood of superstition, all that was left of an adult life of nagging doubt, all that was left of the legacy of fear in the wake of Roger's drowning.

This, and an unholy mess in her life, which would never have come about in the first place if she'd known the truth. If she had, she would have removed her clothes on that first night with Seth. She was glad she hadn't. He'd probably have tried to pay her off with expensive gifts, and she'd have felt doubly soiled for having given in to him.

Suddenly, as surely as if Danielle Fielding had told her what to do, Danny knew how she was going to deal with Seth Whitlaw. She looked upward. "We'll teach him a lesson he won't soon forget, won't we?"

She threw her head back and started to laugh. It was a mirthless laugh that soon dissolved into tears. She covered her face with her hands. Crumpled on the floor at the feet of her great-great-grandmother, for a long time she wept broken-heartedly, with only the far, sad eyes to watch her.

Chapter Twelve

$\mathcal{D}$anny was fated to speak to Seth Whitlaw one more time before her week's deadline came due. It was a short, inconclusive, unplanned meeting in a public place, a bank in the town of Nantucket. Danny went in first thing Monday morning to advise the manager, a man long known to her, that she was expecting a large check. She wanted to know how quickly it could be processed.

Seth was waiting outside the manager's office as she emerged from the inner sanctum, politely escorted to the door by the manager.

At first glimpse, Danny thought Seth was drawn and tired looking, but the moment he caught sight of her familiar face, his features turned to stone.

They drew up facing each other, both halting automatically from the simple unexpectedness of the encounter. The manager's presence, as he turned from

189

one customer to the other, made it hard to ignore the meeting. Danielle nodded coolly. "Mr. Whitlaw," she said.

"Mrs. Morrow," Seth acknowledged stiffly.

"Why, yes, of course you two must know each other. East Widow and Middle Widow. Well, well. Would you wait a moment please, Mr. Whitlaw? I have to arrange for someone to look after Mrs. Morrow."

That left Danny and Seth facing each other. Danny wasn't anxious for the encounter, but she didn't see any reason to avoid it, either. Knowing her day would dawn, she didn't believe Seth could hurt her now.

"The other night you gave me a warning," she said quietly, "but you didn't tell me what would happen if I can't meet your terms. What is it you have in mind? The law?"

His face was impassive. "Are you hoping I'll say no? You'll have to suffer till Thursday, Danielle. We'll talk about the exact consequences when the day of reckoning comes."

Danny allowed her nostrils to flare in the smallest degree, returning some of the scorn he'd showered on her. "That sounds as though you're not thinking of the law. If you were, you'd have no reason to keep me in suspense. Have you decided on some . . . other consequence? Perhaps to do with getting something you've wanted all along?"

As she turned away, ostensibly to study a wall calendar, she was glad to see that Seth looked more than a little sick.

A short time later Danny was at the ferry docks. Forearmed with the knowledge that Jesse Horowitz would be leaving for Boston at the start of the week, and knowing the ferry hours, she could guess the time of his departure. Seeing his Chevrolet already lined up to drive on, she ran and stopped him long enough to hand over a box containing the ruined painting and the various bits and pieces of evidence concerning its origins. "I've made an appointment for you to see a curator at the Boston Museum," she told Jesse breathlessly. "Check his credentials, if you like. I explained the problem."

"Mrs. Morrow, it's not necessary to have that painting examined at all. I don't believe Seth intends to pursue the matter."

"But *I* do. Please go and see the curator," Danny urged. "The appointment's early Thursday morning— here, I've written out all the details. Just *do* it, Jesse. Please."

He looked at her uncertainly, but he took the box. "You're very sure of yourself, Mrs. Morrow," he said slowly. "I have to conclude that Seth's made a bad mistake."

"Yes, he has. You can see part of the evidence with your own eyes if you have a look at the painting. Do it carefully and don't disturb the packing. It's ruined, yes, but it's the same one, and there are photographs that will help prove it. I'm still not sure whether it's a forgery or not, but at the moment that's not the point. I only want to show that it's the same painting, that there could have been no substitution. And if you handle it, Seth can't accuse me of rigging the tests. Would you . . . would you do me a great big favor, Jesse? If you're talking to Seth on the phone, don't mention this. Don't tell him what you're doing until after you've been to the museum. That's a small request, isn't it, after the things he's accused me of?''

A car was honking, warning Jesse to move along. ''I don't know, Mrs. Morrow. I—''

''Thanks,'' she said, and gave him a hug through his car window. As Jesse drove off she could have sworn she saw a blush creeping from his beard up toward his bald pate. She could only hope she had convinced him. Seth's deadline was not until later in the week, and she didn't want him to start questioning his conclusions yet.

Clive Hamilton flew in the following day. Danny met him at the Nantucket airport, and the warmth of the greeting testified to the depth of their friendship. Her affection for Clive was of long standing, even though she'd never returned his one-time amorous interest.

He was a distinguished-looking man, very fit and lean, with graying temples and a high, intelligent forehead. He had come with a briefcase and one small overnight bag, enough to last him until his outgoing flight left in the morning.

As they drove to the Three Widows the inconsequential chatter about old times spared Danny from dwelling on Seth's reaction to her having a male overnight guest. She was forced into awareness of it, though, upon her arrival home. Seth was about to get into his car as the station wagon drew in. He straightened and watched for a moment, his face impassive. Then, without a single sign of greeting, he knifed into his car and took off at a roar.

"Nice neighbor," Clive remarked dryly. "Doesn't he ever smile?"

"Not very often," Danny conceded, and suddenly realized it was true nowadays. She hadn't seen Seth's smile, that warm, outgoing smile that had attracted her in the first place, for weeks. At this point she didn't think he was bestowing it on other women either. She hadn't seen the little Japanese car for several days, not since the night Seth had accused her of working a confidence game.

Danny had supposed there would be reaction on the part of Mildred Merriweather, and she was right. Minutes after she led Clive into her home, overnight bag in hand, Mildred's disapproving face appeared at the door.

"I've come for a cup of sugar," she announced, marching straight for the kitchen when Danny admitted her. As Clive was in the study, looking over his purchase, Danny followed Mildred, feeling mildly irritated.

The lecture started as soon as they were alone in the kitchen. "I see you've started locking up, young missie, so I can't walk in. I suppose you think what goes on behind closed doors is nobody's business but your own? Not three days since you learned the truth, and already you're about to bite the forbidden fruit and let the serpent into the Garden of Eden."

Danny's nerves were a little frayed, so she answered Mildred more sharply than was her wont. "You're right, Mildred. What goes on behind closed doors *is* nobody's business but my own."

Mildred drew herself up in righteous indignation. "I

knew Em should have kept her silence. Well, I'm here to tell you that—"

"I know what you're here to tell me, Mildred. There's no need. I heard it all, years ago. You may as well know right now, my guest is going to sleep here overnight. And I don't want to hear another word about it."

Mildred looked so betrayed and indignant that Danny began to repent her sharpness. More gently she said, "If *you* were behind closed doors with a man, Mildred, would you automatically carry on? Well, I won't either."

"Hmmph," Mildred said, but she had been thrown off the attack.

"He's only come to buy the Sargent, Mildred. Believe me, he's not the Devil incarnate. He's a nice man, a good father to his children, and—"

"Why isn't his wife with him?" Mildred asked suspiciously. The portrait's sale didn't concern her, when there were frailties of the flesh to be worried about.

"Mr. Hamilton is a widower. He has been for years."

"Widower?"

"Don't fret, Mildred. I've known him for ages, because he's a senior partner in the firm Roger used to be with. I saw a lot of him after Roger died, and in all this time he's never tried anything."

"Always a first time," Mildred said dourly, but without her usual spirit.

"Clive is going to sleep in the guest room, Mildred. He's a true gentleman. He would never, never take advantage. Now come and meet him."

Clive Hamilton, with his Wall Street manners and his reserved cordiality, had a reassuring sense of solidity about him. He also treated women very respectfully, and because of Mildred's advanced age he was particularly deferential. He survived her piercing cross-examination with flying colors. When Mildred left Middle Widow, she dropped a very cautious hint that she herself might have picked just such a suitor for Danny, although she disapproved as deeply as ever about the visit. In no uncertain terms, Danny refused the offer of an overnight chaperone. Offended, Mildred delivered some crisp words in parting, all regarding the need for moral fiber.

"Tonight, stiffen your backbone," she advised.

"Believe me, Mildred, I will," Danny said dryly. Then she grinned, as a wicked imp beckoned her into mischief. "If I find myself weakening, I'll simply think of you lying like a sword between us."

Mildred, like Queen Victoria, was not amused.

Twenty-four hours later Danny was ready for Seth. Her negotiations at the bank had been made easier because Clive, who knew she was in a hurry for the money, had thoughtfully provided her with a certified check.

The portrait was to remain at Middle Widow for the time being. Danny had been prepared to arrange for its crating and shipping at once, but Clive had told her there was no hurry. "I wouldn't know what to do with it," he had said. He'd been in touch with the auction house of Sotheby's, who would be sending an appraiser before putting the large Sargent on the block. In time, when all the arrangements were made, the canvas would go directly to them.

With her house guest departed and all details attended to, in the afternoon Danielle went for a long, leisurely swim and was pleased to find that all her old pleasure in the occupation had come back. Slipping into the sea was no longer an exercise in courage; it was an exercise in relaxation. She rolled onto her back in the water and simply enjoyed the sensation of sun drying the beads of moisture on her closed eyelids, while buoyant salt water supported her backbone. Mildred might be in disagreement, but Danny thought that what she was going to do that night would take considerably more backbone than *not* doing it.

And now she had only to wait for nightfall. . . .

Before it came, Danny had soaked away the salt in a warm tub, scented herself subtly, washed her hair and brushed it until the waves cascading over her shoulders shone like the stirred embers of a fire. She was pleased that a few days of rest and quiet, along with firm inner decision, had wrought wonders for her once-exhausted body. She was also pleased that her sunburn had faded to warm gold, with very little evidence to show that her arms had peeled. She ate a small, light supper for sustenance, and then, as the sun slipped low on the horizon, she clothed herself for the evening in a garment purchased in town at the sacrifice of some of her hard-earned dollars. Ready, she sat down in her study to wait for the coming of dark.

As always, she tried to take strength from the ancestral portrait on the wall. It was Wednesday evening, a week short a day since Seth's ultimatum, and Jesse Horowitz's appointment at the museum was scheduled for the following morning. Danielle thought he must have respected her request for silence. Otherwise there would have been some reaction from Seth.

"And there will be, tomorrow," she promised the silent portrait. "I swear he'll remember tonight for the rest of his life. You'd have done it too, wouldn't you? In exactly the same way."

When darkness descended over the Three Widows, and the only night sounds came from hidden crickets and the softly rolling sea, Danny picked up the phone in her study.

"Seth? May we talk?"

His heavy silence was followed by a curt, "Go ahead."

"May I come over?"

"No. The telephone's safer."

"I have to speak to you in person. It's about—"

"I can guess what it's about. You can't meet the deadline tomorrow." The words were flat. "I've been expecting you to phone ever since I saw you at the bank."

"What did you think I was trying to do? Make up the shortfall between the value of your painting and . . . what I received when I sold it?"

She could hear the short, sharp intake of his breath, could imagine that he was steadying himself. "You admit it, then," he said at last. But his voice sounded dull and held none of the triumphant anger she had expected.

"I'd like to explain more about my side of it, Seth. I have to see you, and it must be tonight. Tomorrow I'll be busy getting ready to go back to New York." That was another decision she had made: not a difficult one, because she knew she wouldn't want to remain on Nantucket åfter this night was through.

"Well, I don't want to see you." He had become fierce, intense. "Not in my house . . . not in yours. You've admitted the truth now, and the truth is what I really wanted out of you. Beyond that, there's no need to explain a damn thing."

Danny's heart dipped and her purpose faltered for a moment, but then she looked up and saw the portrait on the wall. "Are you condemning me without a full trial, Seth? I have a story to tell you, a story about my family."

"If it's a sob story, I don't want to hear it."

"What are you afraid of, Seth? That you'll weaken in some way if you see me in person?"

He didn't answer that.

Danny tried again. "If you'd rather, we can meet on neutral territory, down by the beach. It's a clear, moonlit night, Seth. Do you really think anything's going to happen with Mildred Merriweather not a hundred yards away? Her eyes will be peeled as soon as she hears our voices."

Gruffly, after another pause, Seth agreed. "Right down by the water, then, in ten minutes."

It was not quite the meeting Danny had visualized, but it would have to suffice. Before going out into the night, she pulled a shawl over her shoulders. It was a paisley shawl of soft fringed cashmere, dainty swirls of blue and green against a background of creamy white. It was vaguely similar in coloring, if not in design, to the shawl in the portrait. She had bought it after a lengthy search, along with the flowing, long-sleeved nightgown she wore. Tonight she wanted to be not Danny, but . . . Danielle.

The moon was full, as it had been a month before, on her first night with Seth. The shawl, a very large one, cloaked her with decency. As Danny picked her way across the terrace, it covered the partial transparency of the nightgown, an old-fashioned style in sheerest cotton lawn. The demure high collar, lace front, and leg-o'-mutton sleeves were not from the era of the portrait, but they served. And the innocence of white helped remind Danny that she deserved none of the accusations that had been leveled at her.

The pure, virginal nightgown created illusions that weren't true, but they were illusions Danielle wanted, not for Seth but for herself.

In the witching hour of night, on a moon-bathed beach, the illusions were beautiful. When Seth arrived at the point of rendezvous, his breath caught and held. She was standing looking out to sea, with a light breeze sifting her hair, winnowing it over the shawl. Around her legs he saw the drift and swirl of wind-lifted white, but night shadows and many folds of fabric had turned the gown opaque. Her feet were bare. He had a sense of déjà vu, as if he were watching a scene that had been played out long ago.

And then he reminded himself that it had been—many, many times. Anne, in any scene protesting innocence, would have worn white too.

Hearing him, Danielle turned. Seth's black clothes almost vanished into the darkness, but his looming shape could be seen outlined against the silver pallor of the beach. His face was shadowed too, veiling his expression. Moon burnished his hair, the most visible thing about him. Danielle felt the physical tug and pull of him as always, but first she wanted to let Seth know why she had refused him a month before. She gathered her shawl more closely. Folded over her, it revealed no secrets, for each would be told in its own good time.

"Seth, I—"

"Before you say anything, Danielle, let me speak. There's no need to go through this exercise. I'm not going to prosecute, demand more money than you can come up with, or expect payment in favors of any kind. I've decided to chalk the whole thing up to experience —rotten experience. Dragging it out with stories I don't want to hear isn't going to remove the bad taste from my mouth. So whatever little act you've planned for tonight, let's forget it, hmmm?"

She looked at him almost pityingly, feeling an empathy she hadn't expected to feel. "Your wife must have hurt you very badly," she said quietly. "She really did sour you on women, didn't she?"

"Not on *women.*"

"Just on certain women?"

"Exactly. Clever ones."

"You never trusted me, did you? Right from the start."

"No. I started wondering about your motives the moment we met—the moment you lent me a hundred dollars. That's an elementary confidence trick, my friend. I recognize all of them by now. I learned them in the school of hard knocks. And that night on the beach. . . . Shall I tell you why I married my wife in the first place? She went through much the same routine. When I first met her, she scrupulously returned a little money she said my father had lent her.

For a time she was only friendly with me, rather aloof. She had been living under my father's roof, but she managed to convince me rather cleverly that she hadn't been . . . involved. In time she went through a lot of heavy breathing—a taste of the passion she was capable of—and then said no. She did that several times, until I was maddened beyond belief. Sound familiar?''

Danny thought of the night she had rubbed herself against Seth, and knew he was thinking of it too.

His mouth had become as thin as a knife. ''If I ever had doubts about your intentions, Danielle—and I did have a few at first—they were all laid to rest when you returned that simple emerald pin so dramatically. Anne tricked me into a proposal by spurning an expensive gift with a similar gesture. It was a new car. She dropped the ignition key into my bowl of soup in a restaurant, and when it came up with a spoonful of clam chowder, she told me she hoped I'd choke on it. Does that remind you of anything? She had a number of other tricks I'm sure you'd recognize. *I* certainly do.''

''But you loved her,'' Danielle said quietly. ''That must have been hard.'' And while she thought about that her eyes turned slowly and sadly to the sea. At that moment she didn't want to prove anything to Seth Whitlaw. Another woman had made him suffer greatly, and perhaps he deserved no punishment for being overcautious and cynical. If their positions were reversed, she supposed she would have felt much as he did.

Seth stirred restlessly, then walked to stand between her slim body and the water. Facing her and the Three Widows too, it was easier for him to remember that other eyes might be witnessing the scene. ''Now, if

you still want to talk, talk quickly, but remember . . .
at this point you may have more to gain by silence.''

Danny's faraway eyes shifted to his tall, taut frame.
"Tonight I don't want to talk about the Watteau at all.
The deadline you gave me is tomorrow. You'll be
getting your painting back then—the very same painting.''

"You managed to buy it back?''

"It's in Boston right now. You'll get a phone call
about it tomorrow. And that's all I'm going to say.''
She paused, and let a different mood seep into her, a
mood that entered her bones through a moon that had
shone unchanged since eons before the time of the first
Danielle. "I have other things to talk about tonight,
Seth. There's a portrait in my house, of a woman who
was one of my ancestors. She looks very much like
me—or rather, I look very much like her.''

"Jesse told me.''

"Did he tell you about the words on the painting?''

"No. He only mentioned that he'd like to go back
and have a closer look.''

"Well, it is easy to miss the words. The letters are
very small and faded, down near the woman's feet.''
Were, she should have said, but in her mind she had
gone into the past. "When I was a little girl, I always
knew those words were there. Time and again I heard
the story of Danielle Fielding. . . .''

She told of the legend, and of how her husband's
death had reinforced it. "I was afraid of water for a
long, long time. I'm not now, but at the beginning of
the summer I was. It was irrational, but remember, I'd
had a very bad experience. I nearly drowned nine years
ago, and then I drifted for a long time at sea, with no

land in sight. Call it superstition, call it terror, call it cowardice . . . whatever the reason, I avoided the water for years. Remember, I lost my father, my husband, and my unborn child all in one day. It was hard not to believe that the sea had marked me too.''

And then she told of the truth that had supplanted the legend, and of the easy way the words had wiped away, erasing the superstition of years. ''By then I'd worked off . . . most of the fear, anyway. And when I heard the true story, that got rid of the last. I swam today and felt only pleasure.''

''I'm glad for that,'' Seth said quietly. He was struggling not to soften. How should he know if she told the truth? Words that had already been wiped away were evidence of nothing. He reflected on the fact that Jesse hadn't noticed the lettering. Had it ever existed at all? The story held together with the facts he knew about Danielle Morrow, but good stories always did. What might she hope to gain by invention?

He thought of the million dollars she'd extracted from some other man, and he thought of his own wretched credulity years before, and the balance scales in his head tipped him into total cynicism. ''Why do you tell me all this?''

''Can't you guess? *The sea shall tear asunder* . . . I wanted you to know why I didn't make love that night a month ago. And now I'm free to make love if I choose. Truly free in my heart, without fear.''

From a little distance they looked at each other, both wary, both aware of each other's attraction. The silence grew, and the spell of the moon seemed to spin a web around them both, binding them to each other.

''Lie with me, Seth,'' she asked simply.

The expression was old-fashioned, almost quaint, but on that night it seemed right. Seth looked at her and wanted her, and the gravitational pull of his own body almost impelled him forward, like the tides pulling the sea. But then he thought of the times she'd tricked him, and of the night she had pretended to sell herself, and he wondered suddenly if she wanted him to make her pregnant, because then she would have a powerful weapon to use against him.

Anne had used that weapon once. She hadn't been pregnant, but she had pretended it, and it was in the flush of jubilation over the news that Seth had signed over some shares, the only gift he could think of that might truly please his intelligent, honest, unacquisitive wife.

There were many ways a woman could use a child, and a person who had executed one unsavory scheme might very well execute another. He used the harsh thoughts as armor to steel his heart, a weapon to combat the damp heat of desire.

"No," he said. But he couldn't move away.

Danielle allowed the shawl to slip slowly away from her shoulders, onto the sand. No folds of fabric covered her breasts, only a layer of fine thin lawn. Through it gleamed the ivory curve of her breasts and the proud shadow of her nipples. There was purity in the delicate tracery of lawn and lace, there was purity in the tiny ruffles and the innocence of white, but there was no innocence in the seducing moongleam of pale, swaying flesh seen through its thinness. The haunting thighs were a dusky secret, half hidden and half revealed . . . tempting, taunting, moving, maddening. They were a witchery to the senses in that warm, soft night so gently stirred by sea breezes.

Seeing her, Seth desired until desire became a seething volcano in his body. The sweat stood out on his brow, sheening his face.

"Lie with me," she asked again, and again he neither left nor consented. Hypnotized, he stood.

Danielle's back was turned to the land and her face was turned to Seth, who stood between her and the sea. She knew of the eyes that might be watching from West Widow, but it was Seth's eyes she must hold. She unfastened the tiny, old-fashioned buttons at her throat and loosened the small hooks that held her narrow sleeves at the wrist.

She parted the front of her gown and eased the tight forearms away, until her arms were freed. "Lie with me," she whispered a third time, while she held the fabric loosely bunched at her breast.

"No," he said harshly.

She let the gown slip away.

With a groan, Seth reached for her, and with reason destroyed he swept her forcefully into his arms. Caution flung aside, all thoughts of old, watching women flung aside, remembrance of another woman's trickery flung aside, he carried his naked temptress through the night, striding for the haven of East Widow.

Chapter Thirteen

Caught in Seth's impetuous embrace, Danielle at once surrendered to sweet sensation, a helpless reaction to her own hunger for love. In the moment of being swept off her feet, she had forgotten the discarded nightgown. As they moved through the night, nectar stole through her limbs, feeding her with forbidden tastes, promising feasts of great pleasure in the arms of the man she loved and desired.

All time was distilled in the present; all yesterdays and all tomorrows had been forgotten in the immediate needs of the now. She moaned softly as he laid her on his bed and came down beside her, raining hectic, tempestuous kisses over her eyes and her fevered face. In this moment no hardness of heart motivated her. She loved him, and she yearned to express her love, and the long night lay ahead. That was enough for now.

Seth lifted his head. One low lamp illumined the

room, and his eyes smoldered recklessly over the ivories and golds of Danielle's nakedness. He too was lost, feeding on his own obsession.

"You brought the moon inside," he whispered, and in that romantic moment the words seemed no more than a simple statement of truth. "You're beautiful, Danielle . . . oh God, you're beautiful."

She twisted her hands into his sun-gilded hair, and the rich male texture of it was marvelous to her fingers. "Kiss me," she murmured, lifting her face, urging him to end the long gazing and satisfy her cravings.

His breath was warm as he claimed her mouth, thrusting inward with easy mastery to drink her eager offering of passion. As his tongue explored, hers responded with like abandon, and his fingers slowly mapped the pale, seductive curve of her breasts.

The kiss was a whirlpool, drawing Danielle ever deeper into the powerful spell he exerted over her senses. The strong hands coursing over her, the hungry mouth avidly devouring her, the lean, powerful length of aroused man pressing closely against her hip: caught in the eddying current that drowned her, these were the only realities she could hold on to.

Still dressed in his night-dark clothes, Seth slid lower in the bed while his parted mouth sought the peaked tips of her nipples, quenching the thirst of a thousand imaginings. With lips, teeth, tongue, fingers, he teased and taunted the erogenous zones, until the buds of her breasts flowered into a desire that sent her hips straining urgently upward against his moving hand. "Love me, Seth," she begged.

"I've wanted to lie with you for so long," he murmured, his voice muffled. "To love you like this, to make you grow mad with need for me, as I've been maddened by you . . . as I've been driven by you . . . as I've been tortured by you . . .''

The moist, sensuous heat of his lips slid lower, and she felt his tongue stab and sear her flesh until fire attacked her limbs, burning into her like a white-hot brand. Her fingers became flame in his hair, twisting tightly and hurtfully as she cried out her need.

And then the center of her could bear the fine torment no more, and she surrendered to his mouth completely as the fire consumed her in long, sweet throes.

Seth held her hips until the shuddering had ceased, and then he stood and swiftly removed his clothes. Weak in the aftermath of release, Danielle watched him, feeling a softer, slower yearning grow in her as the bronze nakedness of his unclothed body took form beneath her eyes. Seth was a large man but well-knit and compact, hard, muscled, magnificent in his arousal. It was difficult to remember that she had reason to hate him, when she loved him so much that her throat and her heart hurt to think of the weeks when she'd denied herself this moment.

The eyes that had been cynical on the beach were not cynical now. They smoked with a far different message as they raked over Danielle's waiting, reclining form. Seth had accepted his inability to fight nature. Having set his foot upon the path to taking what he wanted, he would now travel the dangerous road all the way to the end, come hell or high water. For the time being, the reckless man and the impetuous lover had taken over from the cynic.

His potent arousal had left him trembling with

urgency as he came down over Danielle, at once gentling her legs apart for possession. The medallion on his neck swung forward to come to rest between her breasts. Blanketing her with his warmth, he murmured, "I wanted to do that first, in case, in case . . . tell me if I hurt you, Danielle."

She understood. Seth was a large man, and she a slender woman. For answer, she wrapped her arms around him, feeling her own power in the rasping unsteadiness of his breath and the breadth of strong sinewy shoulder tensing beneath her fingers.

His kiss, as he took her mouth in a seal of his intention, was tender and deep and slow, and even then he waited until she signaled readiness by sliding her hands to his hips. Once she had pressed him close, he entered carefully.

He lay still for a moment. "Are you all right?" he muttered against her ear.

"Yes," she whispered, glorying in the great potency of his body and the fullness of her own. "Yes, yes, yes."

She had been satisfied once, and he had not. And yet, he began not with his own pleasures, but with hers. His lips toyed gently with her earlobe, wooing her onward for a journey into eroticism in which he would accept no less than her total response . . . again.

He began to move, and the feel of him was a broadsword sheathed in softest velvet. Her body received him, gloved him as if she had been made for his power. Her hips undulated to the gentle rhythm, parrying his thrusts by straining upward to draw him gradually deeper.

His hands worshipped her breasts and his lips praised

her beauty with murmured endearments, until a time
came when the groaning depth of his kiss allowed no
more words. Then his mouth devoured her, fitting over
hers hungrily, moving on her with avid urgency, no
longer asking but demanding. With the little sobs deep
in her throat, with the twisting lift of her hips, with the
movements of her hands on his spine, she told him she
was ready too.

His fingers slid rapidly the length of her body,
shaping her waist, capturing her hips. Powerfully
excited, commanding her fully with the dual force of
mouth and manhood, he clasped her hard against him
as he drove them both relentlessly toward the brink.

They met the climactic moment together. In that fine
ecstasy, with Seth shuddering heavily in her arms,
Danielle almost felt that the planets had altered course,
that the stars had exploded, that the sun and the moon
had mated.

She floated back to her own body and found she was
where she wanted to be, earthbound, locked in Seth's
embrace. He was spent too, still a throbbing part of
her. Her flesh felt like candlewax that had been melted
by his strong flame, then poured to the shape of him.
Even as she gradually solidified again, with passion
receding, she knew she was altered forever. He had
satisfied her utterly, both in the giving and in the
taking.

She knew then that she could not exact her small
measure of revenge. She would accept tonight, welcome it as a gift of fate in exchange for all those wasted
years, and then simply walk out of Seth's life. If he
came after her when she learned the truth about the

Watteau, then so be it. And if he didn't . . . so be that too. But she couldn't insult him as she had intended to do, wittingly and hurtfully, when his consideration in lovemaking touched her so deeply.

In silence, with her mouth buried at his neck, she savored the delicious knowledge of what a wonderful lover he had been. Occasionally, she licked him to taste his salt tang. Occasionally, he inhaled the scent of her hair and stroked its softness. And in time, for her ears alone, he began to breathe the erotic words that described the satisfaction she had given him. They were the words of sex, not of love, but to Danielle it didn't seem to matter. As they lay there twined together in nakedness, there was no denying that the sex had been good, just as Seth was telling her.

"Sinfully good," he muttered, and suddenly Danny laughed.

Abruptly Seth released her and sat up, the medal on his chest swinging hard with the forcefulness of the movement. His eyes narrowed into sudden suspicion as he looked at her. She was stretching indolently, smiling up at him with laughter in her eyes.

"What is it?"

"I was just thinking of the beach, that's all, and who might have been watching. Can't you imagine the shock waves over at West Widow? What a time they'll be having, discussing my behavior. Talk about sins!"

Seth relaxed, and his mouth took on the confident, sensuous, warm smile Danny hadn't seen for so long. The edges of his eyes crinkled attractively. Indolently, he rolled onto his back and pulled her over him. His fingers threaded into her hair to hold her head motionless above him, so that her hair cascaded forward and spilled against his furred chest.

"I've thought about this too often, my beautiful Madame Morrow, to worry about old women's gossip." His voice was lazy, a deep drawl that promised he was not yet through with his lovemaking. "Now that I have you here, I intend to investigate all of your transgressions much more thoroughly than two old women will ever do. We have all night, Danielle, and now that we've started I'm in no hurry to stop. In fact, now that I'm in no hurry at all, I can think of a lot of lovely, wicked, wanton things to do . . . all of them very slow."

He moved her head ever so gently, so that the very tips of her hair grazed and tantalized his chest. With his other hand, he started to stroke her naked hip.

"Now start showing me all your other sins," he growled softly.

Danny woke to find herself warm with a great lassitude, cocooned against Seth inside a single sheet. Her head was snuggled into the crook of his arm, with the sheet draped over her face to shut out the sun that streamed in an open window. With her eyes open beneath the thin covering, she could detect the golden daylight filtering through. She could see Seth's chest hidden in the same shadowy cocoon, the even rise and fall of it, the dark glint of the medal against his skin.

Happiness was a warm glow inside her. She didn't move, simply because she wanted to enjoy Seth's closeness and the marvelous aliveness of her skin. Her nipples were tender and her thighs tingled from too much love, and she didn't mind. How could there be such a thing as too much love, when for too long there had been too little?

She lay still for a long time, because she knew that Seth had been awake far longer than she. Near two o'clock in the morning, at her request, he had gone down to the beach to collect her discarded nightgown and shawl. She had dozed off in his absence, then woken with a start some hours later. The room had been dark, but the lighted dial of a bedside clock had told her the time. It had been well after five and nearing dawn. And no Seth beside her.

But then she had seen him standing naked at the window, brooding in the darkness. Watching him, loving him, she had drifted peacefully back to sleep. The passions shared in the long night, fueled by Seth's stamina, had taken their toll. "I have to prove that I can master you in at least one way," he had whispered at one point, and the responses he had drawn from her had left her enervated, overslaked, whimpering with content.

At some hour, she didn't know when, he had joined her in the bed. It seemed to signal acceptance, as if he had come to grips with whatever difficult thoughts he had been thinking as he stood by the window. Had he been regretting the passion they'd shared?

How could he regret it, when he'd told her in low whispers that no woman had ever satisfied him as she had done? Even if he still questioned many of her motives, he would have to admit to himself that she had given herself fully and freely and with great abandon, asking and expecting nothing but his passion in return.

Finally she could bear temptation no longer. She leaned over and gently bit the tiny hard tip of a flat male nipple. She emerged laughing when Seth flung the sheet away, glowering at her. "That's a helluva way to wake a man," he grumbled.

"I'm hungry. That happened to be the closest part of you." Gradually her grin melted. Her eyes clouded into an expressive, yearning warmth that revealed too much of the depth of her feelings. "Oh, Seth," she whispered, and the tremor in her voice was almost a confession of love. Certainly, it was a tribute to the way he had reawakened her sleeping womanhood.

There were no similar concessions in the enigmatic eyes that met hers. Seth simply looked at her with a coolness she didn't understand, and she felt her blood start to chill.

"I'll get you something to eat, then," he said at last. The words were a little clipped. He swung his legs off the edge of the bed and started to pull on the trousers and sweater he'd discarded the night before.

"I don't want food," Danny said quietly. "I'll go home for that." A quick glance at the bedside clock told her it was nearly noon, an hour when she would prefer not to be here. She wanted to leave at once, and not only because Jesse Horowitz might be phoning from Boston at any moment. With every intuitive bone in her body, she knew that she had been wrong in one thing. Seth still did have the power to hurt her—and after last night he had the power to hurt her as he'd never hurt her before.

"Where did you put my clothes?" she asked.

Silently he handed them to her, and silently he watched as she started to negotiate the narrow forearms of the sleeves. A nightgown was no outfit to wear at this time of day, but it was her only option. With the shawl to cover her and a matter of only fifty yards to go, she would manage. She only hoped the local Legion of Decency, as exemplified by Mildred Merriweather, wouldn't be waiting on the doorstep of Middle Widow. At the moment, with Seth watching her in a way that caused her fingers to tremble, the thought couldn't even raise a smile.

She was still fumbling to put an arm through one of the sleeves when Seth spoke. "If you happen to get pregnant," he said evenly, "I'll take responsibility—*if* the child is mine. First, of course, I'll want blood tests."

She looked up, shocked. "You can't mean that," she whispered.

"I'd have to insist. You were with a man the night before last. Well, is there a likelihood of pregnancy? Did you take precautions or not?"

Danny stared until she could find strength to speak. The rage flowing through her soon provided it, and her voice shook with the intensity of her emotions. "If you were so averse to the idea of fathering a child, you should have asked at the time. And in answer to your question, no, I didn't take precautions, not last night . . . *nor* the night before. You're right, that leaves the question of paternity way up in the air, doesn't it? So I guess if there's any pregnancy, it's my responsibility and mine alone."

Her fingers fastened on the folded piece of paper that had been concealed in the nightgown's sleeve. Holding it restored a determination she'd lost for a time in the loving embraces of the night before. She felt like cold steel, tempered to great hardness by the furnace of emotion Seth Whitlaw continually subjected her to.

Seth's eyes grew concerned. "Backtrack a minute," he said quietly. "I'm not telling you I'm averse. I'd *want* the child, if there was one. And I did think of asking about the possibility last night, but decided the whole thing was worth the risk."

"You think I'd . . . use a child to extract something from you?" Her voice was strangled.

He hardened perceptibly. "It's a common enough routine. And it did strike me that you've had a week to choose your night. Well . . . do you think you might get pregnant?"

Staring, disbelieving, she licked her lips. "Why not? It was an absolutely perfect time of the month. Naturally I arranged it that way."

"When did you get the idea, Danielle? When I saw through your ruse with the painting? No wonder you asked me if I intended to take payment in favors! That would have made it much easier for you, wouldn't it?"

"Yes," she said, because she hoped that would hurt him as he had hurt her. "Much, much easier." *Because I could hate you more.*

"I thought so." His voice was a knife, cutting her to the quick. "Well, for once, my pretty schemer, I'm willing to go along with your scheme. If there is a child, and if it's mine, I'd want it whatever the cost. I'm not talking about giving you support—I'd pay much more handsomely if you gave any child into my care. But remember, there are limits to what you can extract. It would help if you'd tell me the exact figure you have in mind."

Danny jerked the nightgown on over her head. She tossed her tangled hair free in a gesture of pure disdain.

Try and get any child of mine, her head screamed, but her lips were tightly compressed. Her fingers, clutching the fold of paper, were shaking with anger. She turned to get her shawl, and while she wrapped it around her shoulders, she managed to mold her face into an expression of outward calm.

Dignified and pale, she walked down the stairs to the front door, trailed by Seth. He had become silent in the wake of his last insulting offer, as if something in Danny's proud bearing had caused him to start doubting himself.

On the threshold Danny turned toward him, her eyes very cool. "Thank you for last night." She waved the slip of paper without unfolding it. "By the way, this is for you. A check. Not in advance, I'm sorry, but at least it is certified."

"There's no need for that. You said the painting was coming back, and—"

"The ruined painting. And I am responsible for its ruination. I always pay my debts."

She shook the check open and pressed it into Seth's hand, and saw the graying of his face as he read the amount. Three hundred thousand dollars, the full insurance value that had been attached to the Watteau. And then the frown started to gather between his brows, and she could almost feel the questions clicking through his head: Is this a check from the Watteau's sale? Is that ruined thing in Boston just a piece of old junk canvas that was substituted for the real thing? Is Danielle Morrow trying to make herself look good, so she can con me some more? What else does she have up her sleeve?

"If you find yourself in pocket," Danny said distantly, "keep the change. If I do get pregnant, I may even decide the night was worth it. And, and . . . if you want a blood test out of any child I might be lucky enough to produce, go whistle in the wind."

She turned, descended the porch steps, and walked away, with Seth staring after her. She went via the driveway, the only route because of the picket fences that prevented walking on the clipped green lawn. Barefoot, she should have been conscious of the sharp gravel underfoot, but she didn't feel a thing. She was halfway to her own home when Seth acted, his agile legs eating the distance so fast that he caught her long before she reached her front door.

"Danielle . . . !"

His fingers fastened over her arm, and she wheeled on him with the righteous fury of a woman not only scorned, but deeply insulted. With every ounce of strength she possessed, her right hand cracked across his face.

"That's in payment for all the other debts I haven't evened up!" she cried. "Now get out of my life . . . and stay out! And if I do have your child, don't ever expect to find out about it—because first you'll have to find *me!*"

In shock, Seth released her. On his cheek, the imprint of her fingers was beginning to come up dull red. He looked severely shaken. "Danielle, come back to the house. We'll talk. When you threaten to walk off and vanish, maybe carrying my child, I have to concede. You win—dammit, you win. I'll marry you."

Danny turned cold as winter, cold to the very bone.

He still thought she was playing games. It was as if he had slapped her too, a thousand times harder than she had slapped him. She turned on her heel and walked toward Middle Widow, too quickly to hear the faint ringing of a phone sounding from the distance, through Seth's opened front door.

Chapter Fourteen

The spare house key wasn't in its usual hiding place. Danny's fingers slid along the ridge of a loose shingle above a window and discovered nothing. The previous evening, with no purse or pocket to carry anything, she had simply locked the house and left her regular key inside, secure in the knowledge that she could always gain entrance with the well-hidden spare.

She glanced over her shoulder, saw that Seth had vanished back into his house. Her brain was numb but capable of reason. She wasn't running from a raving madman, she knew. She felt very calm. There was no need to dramatize the plight of being locked outside in a nightgown.

Only two other people knew where the key was kept. At least one of them must have used it. Knowing what must wait for her inside, another lecture on original sin,

Danny felt tiredness suddenly weighing on her, a great exhaustion like a stone. Her mind was capable of accepting no more accusations from anyone.

She didn't have to ring, because watchers had been observing through the window. Mildred opened the door. Behind her in the hall of Middle Widow was Emma's worried face, and the weepy expression she wore was a contrast to Mildred's hatchet features.

"We waited up for you all night," Mildred accused grimly as Danny stepped inside.

"Although we did sleep a little," Emma said, sounding apologetic and teary. "I used the blue guest room, I hope you don't mind, Danny, and—"

"Em! Hold your tongue. Only one person needs to account for herself today, and it's clear as day that's not you. Wearing nighties at noon, indeed! And *not* wearing them at night! Well, young missie? What do you have to say for yourself?"

The lecture triggered a total closing of Danielle's mind. She hardly heard it. The need for self-protection saved her from becoming overwrought. Attacked by Mildred, at once she wrapped her feelings into a heavy haze where nothing could touch her. It was as if her private, personal self had suddenly vanished into one of the heavy fogs that sometimes obscured Nantucket Sound.

No one could see through that fog, not even Danielle herself. It enveloped her totally. Her calmness became complete. She went past the Merriweather sisters as if they were invisible, walked upstairs, locked herself in the bathroom. She felt almost invisible herself. She was cold to the marrow. She ran a hot tub and lay in it, wondering abstractedly why those nuisance voices kept calling things through the door. She heard the doorbell ringing again and again, and that was a nuisance too. She heard shouts. She heard a banging noise somewhere. She heard whispers. Then more voices and rattlings at the bathroom door. She didn't know the reason. Noises kept happening, and she wanted them all to stop.

In time it came to her that the bath was chilled, and she wondered vaguely why she had run it that way.

She stepped out and dried herself very precisely, with great care. She didn't want to put her nightgown on again. With dignity, she opened the door and walked naked to her bedroom. This time she didn't see Mildred or Emma at all. They didn't seem to exist. She was only aware that a blessed silence had fallen over the house in the exact moment of her emergence.

She dressed slowly, automatically taking the clothes Emma handed her, not knowing where they came from. The murmurs and mutters swirling around her ears distressed her, and she closed her mind to what they meant. She was still cold, so she took a heavy sweater from her drawer and a heavy blanket from her bed, not seeing the worried glances exchanged behind her back. It was a very hot day, and that type of bundling shouldn't be needed.

She dragged the blanket downstairs, located the key to her study, and went in. She locked the door behind her so no one could follow, and then she wrapped the blanket around her body and sat down.

The fog served its purpose, cushioning the worst of her feelings, insulating her against further hurt. Faint sounds reached her from time to time. Voices coming from a great, great distance . . . women's voices . . . then a man's voice . . . she distantly knew it was Seth, but she didn't want to talk to him. It couldn't be important. Then there was a phone ringing right by her elbow, ringing again and again, until she took it off the hook. Seth's voice came through the receiver. She hung up, then lifted the receiver to break the connection before it could ring again. The phone was like a foghorn interrupting her peace, and she didn't want to hear it.

In time the telephone began to emit an unpleasant whine, and she couldn't think how to stop it. Eventually she pulled the cord right out of the wall. She was too cold to listen to a disturbance like that.

Danielle was in emotional shock, although she didn't know it. She had no notion of how long she was in the study. Once in a while she took a drink of water in the small attached bathroom, and once in a while she washed her face and her hands in very hot water. The water steamed and burned her skin but she still felt chilled. After a time it grew dark, but she didn't bother turning on a light. In the gloom her head started to nod, and her beleaguered body told her that she needed sleep. She lay down on the floor and huddled into the blanket, shivering. The floor didn't seem too uncomfortable, but she vaguely wondered why she had lain down in the study and not in her bed. Then she recalled that it was because she was locked in. It all seemed quite logical.

If only those voices would stop buzzing outside the door.

If only she could remember exactly what had happened today.

If only she weren't so cold.

She woke with a start to all hell breaking loose. Someone was trying to pry the door open and the burglar alarm had gone off. Almost instantly she understood exactly what was happening, for the great restorative of sleep had ended her confusion. She knew why she was here, she knew whose voices she heard in the hall, and she knew whose hands were trying to force the door.

This was one attempt at break and entry that was not deterred by the loud, incessant whine of the burglar alarm. Seth kept trying, with the voices of the two Merriweather sisters to encourage him in his efforts.

Alert but unable to see in the dark, it took Danny a few moments to find a light switch. A clock told her it was still quite early in the evening; she supposed she had slept for no more than an hour. Calmly, she went and opened the door. Seth, in the act of straining against a crowbar, froze.

Danny switched off the burglar alarm, and the sudden silence was deafening.

Emma and Mildred were both very upset. They began to fuss, crowding around Danny to assure themselves that she was all right. She was; but she permitted their flow of questioning for the simple, sound reason that it prevented Seth from reaching her. He was standing in the background with a pained expression on his face and the crowbar hanging loosely in his big hands. For once he looked helpless, as if he wasn't sure what to say or do.

Before many minutes had passed, the alarm's relay system brought police sirens. More questions, more confusion; and in the ebb and flow of people Danny managed to remain aloof from the one person she didn't care to talk to.

At last the police, two of them, completed their detailed report. "Will you be all right, then, Mrs. Morrow?"

"Certainly," she said. "As I told you, I was only severely overtired. I'll be fine now."

The officer in charge frowned, once more taking in the paleness of her face and the signs of strain. "Under the circumstances, possibly it's best if you're not alone until you've had a decent rest. Going to sleep in the bathtub could have had serious results, and then not remembering that you had ripped out the phone. . . . Perhaps one of your neighbors would be good enough to stay with you for the night."

Danny turned to Mildred and Emma. "Would you?" she asked.

Moments later, when the officers were at the door, Danny looked at them and gestured pointedly in Seth's direction. "Would you be kind enough to show this gentleman back to his front door? I wouldn't care to lend him a flashlight, in case he neglected to return it." She smiled faintly. "He's that kind of neighbor."

The police laughed, but Seth didn't. His face was totally expressionless. But as he went out the door, his scowl became unsettling, and so did the look of grim determination on his face.

There were no more lectures for Danny. Earlier, Mildred had expended all of her verbal energy on empty air, and concern had long since replaced outrage and chagrin. With irresolution knocking some of the stiffness out of her, she looked a little more like Emma tonight.

Emma tucked Danny into bed while Mildred vanished to the kitchen. "I love him, Emma," Danny said, because she didn't want Emma to be upset by anything she'd witnessed. Emma kissed her and gave a watery smile and then buried her face in a handkerchief.

Mildred had gone to the kitchen to prepare hot broth, her answer to illnesses of every origin. Danny accepted it gratefully and managed a few wan smiles. "I love him, Mildred," she said then too. Mildred turned her head away for a minute, pretending she had something in her eye. "But it won't stop me from making you a boiled egg," she offered smartly, in case anyone thought she was weakening.

Danny refused, and soon she was left alone in the blessed silence of her own room.

She lay with her eyes open in the dark, wide awake now. In time even the quietest of murmurs ceased, and the thin line of the hall light vanished from beneath her door. Soon the faint sound of a snore reached her— Mildred was not a quiet sleeper. In time, when Emma didn't creep downstairs for hot cocoa, her habitual cure for insomnia, Danny judged that both the sisters would be asleep.

She waited another hour to be sure. Then, very silently, she rose from her bed, switched on a low light, and dressed. She imagined Seth would be knocking at the door in the morning, and she wanted to be gone by then.

Many decisions had been made during the long, silent wait in bed, so it wasn't hard to prepare for departure. In coming to Nantucket, she'd brought only a few casual summer clothes, most of which wouldn't be needed in New York. She would simply abandon them. Over the summer she'd also worn some clothing left in mothballs nine years before; Mildred would undoubtedly return everything to mothballs in time. And if she didn't, Danny didn't care. The clothing could be thrown away by the new owners, when Middle Widow was sold. To sell had been one of her decisions.

The only important things in her bedroom were her handbag and some small family pictures. She removed some nonessentials from the former in order to make room for the latter and, in total darkness, crept quietly down the stairs.

There were no canvases to be packed in the car. They'd all been returned during Danny's last trip to New York. The various professional necessities—camera equipment and reference books and tacking irons and surgical tools and microscope and a hundred other oddments—would have to be left behind, she had decided. There was far too much to transport easily. The things could be picked up by a mover, provided they were put in proper order. A good part of the next two hours was spent in doing just that.

The only things she wanted to take with her were a few of the more portable family treasures, small mementoes whose history far outweighed their monetary value.

Very silently, in sock feet and semidarkness, she set about gathering them together. Some small ivories

from the scrimshaw collection. A sextant. The astrolabe. An old compass and a navigation chart that had
belonged to Jethro Fielding. A handful of valued
books. One of them was a slim volume of French
poetry that had been owned by Danielle Fielding
herself. *Poèmes Saturniens*. Danny located it on a top
shelf. The soft, much-handled suede cover had crum-
bled at the edges, and the gilt lettering showing the
name of the poet, Verlaine, had almost worn away.
Inside, in ink faded by time to palest brown, there were
tiny, flowing notations in the margin, in Danielle
Fielding's own script.

One cardboard box held everything, with room to
spare, while some toxic solvents she didn't dare trust to
the movers went into an old camera case she had
converted for the purpose.

She sat down at her desk and wrote a long letter to
Emma and Mildred. She thanked them for their care
and concern, told them to help themselves to the
supplies in the kitchen and the refrigerator, and informed them that she would be selling the house
immediately through an agent. She asked them to admit
movers, whom she would contact, in order to pick up
the items now neatly packaged in the study. She also
explained, in some detail, the arrangements that had
been made for the disposal of the Sargent portrait, and
requested that they admit the evaluator who would be
coming from Sotheby's.

She could think of no more to say. Except . . .

I love you both very dearly. I wonder if you know
how much? I'll be phoning you from time to time,
as always. I don't think I . . .

At that point she paused. How could she write "I don't think I could bear my life if you weren't in it"? Emma and Mildred would worry. It wasn't true, anyway. There were many reasons to bear life—good friends, good people, good memories mingled with the bad. There was even the chance, admittedly not a certainty, that the seed sown in passion might at this very moment be creating new life and new hope inside her. Danny wielded her pen again.

I don't think I would have caused you so much trouble if I'd listened to you better, Mildred. Emma, in case you're looking for your lucky penny again, you left it in my bedroom. Hugs to both of you. Love . . .

She looked up at the portrait on the wall and then signed herself as Danny. If there was one thing she was not, it was her ancestress Danielle. She wondered how she could have slipped into that role so completely the night before, even to the extent of removing her clothes for all eyes on a bright, moonlit beach.

She was ready. She wouldn't leave the house until she could see her way, and even then she would not leave the Three Widows until she had to. Starting the car offered too great a risk of waking others. She would stow her few belongings without even closing the station wagon door, then simply sit and wait until she saw the first stirrings at either of the houses. With luck, it wouldn't come until near ferry time. Then she would simply take off. She wouldn't be able to get a ferry berth for her car at this late date, but she needed it to transport the few things she was taking. She would leave the car locked up in town and collect it at some future date.

She sat through the night and waited for dawn, living with the portrait, regretting, but no longer regretting everything. From time to time her hand gentled the concave hollow of her stomach, wondering, marveling, that there might be even the smallest possibility of something she had once considered well nigh impossible.

Before the first light stained the sky, she realized that if she had it all to do over again, she would probably do most of it in exactly the same way.

"Particularly the last part," she murmured to Danielle Fielding. She walked to the portrait, as if it were a real person to whom she must make her final adieux. She raised her fingers, reaching across time to touch those other fingers. . . .

Untouched, untouchable let her be

Danny lowered her hand without touching anything. One wasn't supposed to leave fingerprints on valuable paintings, anyway. The oils always present on the surface of human skin damaged the oils of a canvas.

"Good-bye," she whispered. She picked up her few possessions and went from the house, quickly and quietly.

Chapter Fifteen

It was still very dim outside, for the sun hadn't risen. Her car was as she'd parked it, nose toward Middle Widow. As it was not a circular drive, she would have to back it out. She scolded herself for not jockeying it into position, ready to leave, as she usually did. But then she remembered that the last time she'd used the car was in driving Clive Hamilton to the airport, and on that day she'd had far more important things on her mind.

She opened the door of the driver's seat very cautiously, careful to make no sudden sound. Silently she eased her burden—one cardboard box, one leather case—across to the passenger side. To open the station wagon trunk, which couldn't be closed without slamming, was an invitation for eyelids to fly open. In city or town such noises wouldn't be noticed, but in the vicinity of the Three Widows one became accustomed

to their absence. Thunder and lightning and a howling
sea wind would attract less attention from sleepers.

Bending into the car, she heard a light clink at the
gravel near her feet. She realized she'd dropped her
ignition keys. It was too small a sound to betray her; all
the same, for a moment she held her breath. Then she
bent, reaching for the keys which lay in full view.

Something caught the corner of her vision. It was
just the faintest outline, no more than a shadow, but it
was enough to send her eyes skidding toward the rear
of the car.

The shadow took form, became a man's legs . . .
and for an instant, as alarm ricocheted through her, she
experienced the same reaction a mother feels to see a
child race across a street with no heed for traffic.

In a few steps she was at the back of the car, looking
down at the driveway with a secondary reaction—
anger—splintering through her. It was Seth. He was
lying on the gravel, still in dark clothes, unshaven,
draped in the sleep of exhaustion, with the length of his
supine body a bar to her departure.

Didn't he know she could have run over him?

Then she started to grow shaky, simply because it
was true.

He slept very deeply, she thought, because she
hadn't remembered to keep quiet during the last few
moments. Her feet had been crunching the gravel quite
loudly.

Caution restored, she went quietly back to the
driver's seat. This time, every tiny crunch of her feet
seemed immense, and she cursed the picket fence that
prevented her from traveling on grass. She slipped
halfway into the seat, perching with toes still on the

ground while she pondered the problem. For a time she could think of no solution at all. She didn't want to face Seth, but she most certainly couldn't drive out without asking him to move. And the bike wouldn't do; its carrier was too small for her parcels. Besides, it was kept in a shed with a squeaky hinge.

But she still had feet, and lots of time to get to town. She would have to abandon the few things she'd placed in the car, but she could always send for them, along with the car itself. Surely someone could be hired to bring it to New York. Yes, she resolved at once: she would walk.

The worst part would be stepping over Seth's ankles on her way to the road. She decided it would be better to go around to the other side of the car and pass by his head. That had risks too, but at least there was a concrete walkway on which the sound of her footsteps would be practically undetectable. She was glad she'd worn slacks and rubber-soled shoes.

A journey of a thousand miles starts with a single step, she reminded herself. And the longer she put it off, and the lighter the sky became, the more likely Seth would be to awaken on his own.

Gathering the strap of her handbag close so it wouldn't flap against her hip, she stood and began her slow progress toward safety. The hard walkway, when she reached it, mercifully ended the tiny sounds that had been made by shifting gravel. When Seth's streaky hair came into view, she breathed one shallow breath of relief to see that he still slept, sprawled face-up in exactly the same way.

And then, as she crept past him, she stopped breathing at all.

Seconds later she had passed the picket fence and the neatly manicured front of Middle Widow. She went faster now. Again avoiding gravel and the road itself, she stepped onto a verge of long wild grass that would muffle her footsteps. A little farther, a little farther . . . and then she was racing, breathing more heavily, no longer so cautious. As she neared the crest of the rise behind which she would soon disappear on her way to the main road, her heartbeat intensified and her hair streamed wildly behind her. She turned in flight, pausing for a last backward glance to make sure Seth hadn't wakened. . . .

He was hurtling at her, and she had the confused impression of a football tackle closing in. She turned in time to see only that much, and then she was beneath him, breath knocked from her lungs, trapped by the press of his powerful body. The grass that had muffled her footsteps had also muffled his.

"I'm sorry," he panted. "If you hadn't stopped just then . . ."

But he didn't release her, and he didn't move his weight from on top. With his superior size and hard-packed body, it was an effective prison.

"Let me go!"

Danny's fists flailed, but he manacled her wrists easily, holding her hands against the grass so she couldn't continue to pummel him. "Not until I've had my say," he warned grimly. "I'll climb off you then, and not before. Might as well save your breath for answering—at least enough to say yes. Will you marry me, Danielle?"

"No!" Panting, she glared at him. "You've had your say. Now get off!"

"I'll rephrase myself. I'll climb off you when you've said yes, and not before. Will you marry me, Danielle?"

"No!"

He sighed heavily. "I guess I'll just have to keep you here until you've found breath for the proper word. I love you, Danielle. Will you marry me?"

"N—"

His mouth descended, making the answer impossible to finish. His unshaven jaw rasped on her skin, but his lips moved over hers tenderly, seductively, arousingly. His tongue dragged and teased and dipped, and the small, leisurely tastes were more tempting than complete mastery would have been. At the same time his thumbs stroked the fluttering pulses at her wrists, caressing them as though they were small birds locked in the prison of his grasp, and he a gentle jailor.

When he at last lifted his face, she forgot to finish the unspoken answer. The expertness of his kiss had weakened her in a way she recognized only too well. There was danger in this moment when they lay together in the long grasses, and the wild beat of her heart warned her that the physical perils were immense. In her weakness for Seth, she had not closed her mouth against the kiss.

She fought to close her heart instead. The warmth of feeling evoked by the extreme tenderness of his kiss told her that the dangers were not purely physical ones.

She remembered the trembling anger she'd felt a short time before. "How dare you go to sleep practically under my car," she said in a choked, shaky voice. "I might have killed you."

He smiled, the warmth of his expression a contrast to

the venom of hers. "You can't get rid of me that easily, darling. I'd have heard the ignition. Anyway, I didn't go to sleep intentionally—I think I drifted off vertical, and ended up horizontal. How are you feeling this morning, sweetheart?"

"Fine! Until you came down on me like a ton of bricks. Please get off."

For answer, he dragged his lips across her throat.

Danny groaned and tried to move, but the crushing size of his body effectively trapped her.

"I love you, Danielle," he muttered, and although her body resisted little, her mind did. How could she allow herself to listen to a man who trusted her so little?

"You want me," she contradicted, defying him with the sparkle of her eyes. "You want *sex*. That's all you wanted, right from the start. Well, you've had one night of it, and you're not having more. I've given you too much of myself already. Now leave me alone."

"Will it help if I confess to those particular sins? I want you. I want sex. I wanted it right from the start. I had one night of it, and I want more . . ." His eyes searched her face, and his voice lowered to a persuasive murmur. "A whole lifetime of nights. A whole lifetime of love."

"That's not love. It's . . . lust. Now get off, Seth! You're heavy."

"No, I won't get off, not until we've had this out. Stop squirming, will you? It does things to my lustful imagination—and yes, I lust for you, I admit it. Is that so unforgivable? Love has to start somewhere, and mine happened to start with wanting to take you into my bed. But now I want to take you into my life, Danielle . . . all of you . . . heart, body, soul. . . .''

Seth freed one of her wrists and stroked a wisp of hair away from her face with such extreme tenderness that she forgot to use her unshackled hand as she ought. ''I'll confess to some more sins too. I'm an easy mark for a beautiful woman like you. For most of this summer I've been too damn busy fighting my own weakness, my own attraction, to see that the real beauty of you goes far deeper than the surface. I've said many wrong things, many untrue things, many cruel things. I wish I could blame all the cynicism on old, bad experience, but I have to take some of the blame on myself. I was afraid to love. Afraid of commitment. Afraid to be hurt. So . . . I tried to hurt you, before you could hurt me as badly as . . . as I myself was once hurt. Perhaps I was even venting some of the old anger at my wife.''

''Why pick on me?'' Danielle cried. ''Why not one of your other women?''

For a moment Seth bent his head to her throat, a posture of humbleness. The sun broke over the horizon, and the sudden gilding of his many-colored hair caused a prickling in her fingertips. She wanted to know its feel again. When Seth looked up, his voice was thickened with emotion. ''Because it was you I fell in love with. Yes, I wanted you the first time I saw you, but I think I loved you from the first time we met. That put a great power into your hands. Then, when you started using it. . . .''

He was doing it again. Danny closed her eyes in pain. Would he never stop accusing her?

"I don't mean that the way you think," he said quietly, and her eyes came open again, colder and harder than before.

"How do you mean it, then? What's my sin this time? Did you happen to miss a silver teaspoon yesterday? I confess, I took it."

Seth looked exasperated. "Sometimes," he said dryly, "I don't think the entire burden of our problem can be laid at my doorstep. It takes two people, pretty lady, to create a problem—and it also takes two to solve it. Trouble is, you're too damn proud. You're also very stubborn. You could have saved us both a whole lot of heartache by telling some simple truths long before now. Or perhaps I should say, defending yourself against the *un*truths I was thinking. If you'd told me the story of your family superstition a month ago, that would have been a good start. Then I wouldn't have thought you were holding out for something. If you'd simply returned the emerald, instead of going through an elaborate routine, I wouldn't have thought you were trying to use yourself for some kind of gain. And if you'd admitted where you got that million dollars . . ."

Danny stiffened as if he had struck her with a whip. "Sending your man over to pump me! That was a low trick!"

". . . then we wouldn't be lying here at dawn, fighting like hell about something we both want. Why wouldn't you tell Jesse where you got it?"

"It was none of his business! Or yours. So if you're still trying to find out, forget it."

"I'm not. I've already found out everything about you. Absolutely everything." Soft laughter crinkled the edges of Seth's tawny eyes. "I'm beginning to understand you very well, darling. When attacked, you don't defend. You attack back."

He smiled down at her, that warm Sungod smile of his, but Danielle ordered her body not to go buttery. "Any confessions you'd like to make," he murmured, "to add to the things I learned about you yesterday?"

Danny resisted the impulse to ask what he had learned, and from whom. She answered stiffly. "No."

Seth made a mock stern mouth. "Most of your prickly pride I can forgive," he growled, "but there's one piece that was just too much. You shouldn't have allowed me to believe you'd been physically involved with your house guest the other night. You could easily have told me he was only there to buy a painting."

"He was there for a good deal more than that," Danny said haughtily. "Clive and I have been involved for years."

"Like hell."

"And how would *you* know? I don't leave my bedroom curtains wide open, the way you do! Now move and let me up."

Seth sighed and ignored the request. "Curtain preference is the first domestic problem we'll have to solve, then. We could settle for a little give and take. I suggest curtains closed against Peeping Toms when we first go to bed, then opened for the dawn."

The mention of Seth's bedroom was intrusive, piercing her defenses. She closed her eyes to shut out his face. "Stop it, Seth. I'm not going to marry you."

"In that case," he said promptly, "I'll give in. Closed curtains all the time. *Thin* closed curtains. One of these mornings, I'll want to make love to you by sunlight, at dawn. Not a bad idea at that. . . ." His hand slid down to her hip and started an insidious stroking. "May I?"

Her eyes flew open. "No! I don't want to."

Seth sighed again, more heavily. His hand moved upward and slid between their bodies to cup a breast. Thoughtfully, between forefinger and thumb, he examined the evidence that betrayed her lie. At once sensitized, her nipple sprang to his fingers. Seth smiled down at her.

"With the various deceits you go through, my good Madame Morrow, it's hard to believe you were brought up by someone as plainspoken as Mildred Merriweather. Thank God she's a little more honest than you, Danielle. Yesterday she handed out more home truths than you can imagine, most of them along with a fearsome tongue-lashing. Actually," he added idly, "I also spoke to your friend Mr. Hamilton, at Mildred's suggestion. I phoned him long distance. Among other things, the righteous Miss Merriweather was trying to find out which of the two of us should be scourged into making you an honest woman."

Danny's heart was pounding very fast. "So that's how you found out I hadn't slept with him!"

Seth grinned down at her, looking very pleased with himself. "Clive Hamilton also told me another big, important thing about you," he muttered. He had raised his chest a little, to allow a lazy flicking of her nipple. With interest, he was watching her reactions.

Danny's mental powers were deserting her. She tried valiantly to remind herself that Seth didn't really trust her for herself alone, any more than he had ever done. Quite simply, he had discovered the truth about her stock market speculations. And by now he'd probably found out that the ruined painting was the same one he'd delivered into her keeping. And a few other things too.

"Please get off me, Seth. It's getting uncomfortable under here."

Indeed, it was, but the discomfort stemmed mostly from the physical responses that were the natural result of prolonged closeness. The full burgeoning of Seth's manhood was no secret now, and Danielle's resolve was dissolving in the fluidity of her thighs. Her head was starting to spin crazily.

Seth freed her other wrist. He twined his fingers into a strand of her hair, held it to his nose, and inhaled. "Odd," he murmured, "I'm not finding it uncomfortable at all. I feel I could stay here all day."

"You're hurting me."

"You're hurting me, by refusing the honest offer of my hand and heart. If you want me to move, say you'll marry me."

"No," she answered, but it was hardly more than a whisper.

Seth bit the ends of her hair softly, holding her with his eyes. He trailed the dampened strand back and forth across her mouth and said lazily, "You want more talk first? Well, I think it's time you fessed up about a few more things." He was looking down at her with the possessive arrogance of a man who knows the prize to be within his reach, and indeed it was. Danny's mouth was parted and her eyes were becoming glazed. "You could begin with the fact that you love me," he suggested.

"I don't," she protested, but it was a weak protest

accompanied by a soft murmur of desire low in her throat.

"That's no way to start a marriage. Isn't it time we came to an understanding, Danielle? Shared a few more secrets?" He blew gently on her eyelids, then described the fine line of her brows with a lingering tongue. His mouth moved with a lover's intimacy to an ear, and his lips nibbled softly, causing her to moan and stir. "I adore you, darling," he murmured. "I've placed all of me in your hands, and I want all of you in mine."

"No . . ."

He punctuated each of his pleas with a shiveringly tender kiss. "Be my woman. Be my mate. Be my helpmeet. Be my comrade. Be my companion. Be my lover. Be my mistress. Be the mother of my children. Be my *wife*. And please say yes very, very quickly. My lustful imagination is giving me hell."

"No," she whimpered.

"That's not good enough, sweetheart." He held her face between both his hands. Tiny, tender kisses rained against her cheeks, her chin, the verges of her hair. "I'm offering you everything this time . . . everything I own."

"No . . . you're *hurting*, Seth."

"My body, my heart, my soul, myself . . ."

"No . . ."

". . . and my trust, *all* my trust."

"No, no, no."

Seth lifted his head. "By the way," he said in a conversational tone, "I didn't know you hadn't slept with Clive Hamilton until you admitted it just now.

And I don't know whether the Watteau is a fake or whether it's the same picture or whether there's a collection of old shoes in that box you gave Jesse. After several days of wondering what to do, he delivered the parcel to the museum without even looking into it, because he didn't want to be forced into taking sides. He didn't stay to find out anything from the curator—he only phoned to tell me what you'd said, and what he'd done, and why he felt he had to opt out of helping you, beyond delivering the whole thing into expert hands. I suspect he didn't tell me until after the appointment because somewhere deep down his sympathies are with you.''

"You don't . . . know?" she whispered.

Seth nodded. "I might have been able to find out the answer yesterday, Danielle—I was supposed to phone the curator. I didn't. You know why? I was too damn busy trying to beat my way past a bodyguard of two formidable old ladies, in order to reach the only person I cared to see.''

She was still trying to assimilate that when Seth went on. "And I still don't know where you got that million dollars. And I don't know a whole lot of other things about you, things I sure as hell can't figure out for myself. And I no longer give a damn, because I know the one important thing—I love you beyond all reason and I trust you beyond all doubt. In the course of a lifetime, I'll find out the answers to the rest. For now, the only answer I need from you is . . . yes.''

A great joy stole into her heart as the full import of his words came to her. "Oh, Seth," she sobbed, throwing her arms around his neck. She hugged him tightly while tears of pure happiness shimmered to the surface and quivered, shining like dew in the tremulous new dawn. "I love you so damn much it hurts."

The stubble of his jaw raked her while he sought to find her mouth. "Say yes and the hurting will stop," he growled in a husky promise.

"Yes," she whispered. And her heart told her: it already has.

Long before the Merriweather sisters awoke, Danielle and Seth had quietly entered Middle Widow—Danny feeling young and pleasurably guilty, for she knew that Mildred's eagle eye could hardly fail to detect the burning after-effects of lovemaking on her face. During the sweet moments stolen in the long grasses, Seth's rakish stubble had taken its toll.

Seth carried the small box of Fielding keepsakes into the house. Upstairs there were no stirrings: it was not yet seven A.M., the hour when Mildred, punctual as a clock, would shake Emma up to start the day.

In the big, homey kitchen Danny brewed coffee, the simple ritual made difficult by the strong arms that kept stealing around her, and by the low love mutters that kept stirring at her ear.

She would have aimed for the kitchen table with the two steaming mugs, but Seth took them both from her hands. "We're taking it in your study," he said firmly. "I want to have a look at my new purchase."

Danny looked puzzled, not comprehending.

Seth grinned mockingly. "It's not every day a man buys a valuable work by John Singer Sargent, sight unseen."

"You bought it from Clive," she whispered,

stunned. As the news sank in, radiance grew on her face. She had thought the great joy of the morning could become no greater, but her full cup of happiness was now flowing over. If Seth had not had his hands occupied with liquid directly off the boil, she would have thrown her arms around him.

In the study Seth stood behind Danielle with his arms locked around the portrait's look-alike, while he admired his acquisition. "She must have been a remarkable woman," he said, "just like you."

"I'm very glad you bought her back," Danny said with heartfelt gratitude.

"I bought her for you, darling, and don't bother telling me you don't accept expensive gifts. I bought her with *your* money, the same money you got from selling her. After everything you told me about Danielle Fielding—and after I realized why you'd sold her—I knew we couldn't let her leave the family."

Mildred, it seemed, had informed him about the portrait's sale. It had come up inadvertently, during a tirade about which of the two men owed it to Danielle to save her honor. "Mildred didn't seem to have any idea about the portrait's worth, but I had a damn good notion. Then it hit me like a thunderclap. *That's where you got three hundred thousand dollars.* Not from selling a Watteau, not from any other source . . . and it also hit me that you'd never, never have parted with your namesake unless you'd been desperate to prove a point of honor. About the time all this was going through my head, Mildred produced the information about Clive Hamilton's occupation, so it was easy to get in touch with him."

"So that's when you started trusting," Danny

mused, snuggling comfortably into her niche in his arms. It seemed right and fateful that the portrait, which in a sense had created much of the trouble, had also helped solve it—as if that Danielle Fielding of old had decided to reach into the present and change the course of two star-crossed lovers. Perhaps it was superstitious to feel that way, but if so, it was a harmless superstition Danny would treasure all her life.

"That was the moment of absolute trust, yes," Seth conceded. "At that point all my preconceived notions about you came crashing down like a house of cards. I knew I had to get the portrait back for you. I had no doubts about you, not one . . . but if I had had, your friend Mr. Hamilton would have mowed the last of them down. I offered him a handsome profit on the transaction and he refused it. If the portrait was going back to Danielle Morrow, he said, he wouldn't dream of speculating. He said he owed you an enormous obligation for something you'd done years ago— paying off a huge debt you weren't legally obligated to pay at all."

Seth turned Danny in the circle of his arms and said seriously, "That was the big, important thing I learned from him, darling. I didn't have to be told what the debt was. I already knew the amount, and I knew the debt was the result of your husband's unwise speculating with clients' money. By then I had a very good idea about the type of woman who would pay off more than a million dollars she didn't owe. The same type of woman who would pay off three hundred thousand she didn't owe." He paused and smiled warmly. "Perhaps even the same type of woman who'd lend a hundred dollars to a man she didn't know."

Danny laid her head against his shoulder, feeling safe there now. "I trusted you on sight," she said. "Perhaps it would have been better if I hadn't. Then my first move wouldn't have been . . . the gesture of a confidence woman."

Seth pretended a strict voice. "From now on I'll have to keep a close eye on your good heart and your honorable motives, darling. With your tendencies, you could go through a fortune very fast."

Danny laced her arms around his neck and smiled up at him, loving him so much that her chest was full to bursting. "So could you! Don't accuse *me* of having a good heart and honorable motives. Shall I tell you when I fell in love with you, Seth? It was when I realized you'd bought out practically a whole store full of bathing suits, simply to make a young, insecure girl feel confident and good about herself. A man who would do that . . . well, even though you were wickedly attractive and far too impetuous and maybe even a little bit unscrupulous with women, and even though you had designs on me, you couldn't be all bad, could you?"

"Yes, he could," came a sharp voice from the doorway.

"Has he proposed yet?" asked a quavery one.

Danny turned, laughing. "Yes, he has. Now turn your back, Mildred, or expect to have your eyeballs sizzled. I'm about to kiss the big lug."

Mildred was outraged. "At seven o'clock in the morning!"

"Oh, how romantic," sighed Emma.

"Emma! Stop looking this very minute! Can't you see they're kissing like the *French people* do?"

Several long, lovely, lazy days later, Seth received the news about the Watteau. It was a forgery, a good one—but very definitely a forgery. No insurance protected against ill chance like that, so the painting was a total write-off. "The worst of it is," he said gloomily, "the same Whitlaw who bought that fake collected a few other things, and maybe some of them came from the same dealer. I suppose they'll all have to be looked at now. It seems my forebears were easy marks, just like me." His glumness dissolved into a rueful grin. "It was worth it though, every penny. If it hadn't been for that painting, you and I might have simply walked out of each other's lives. And I hated it anyway. All the same, it would have been nice if the old dog who bought it had exercised a little better judgment in the treasures he acquired."

Suddenly Danielle remembered about the box of Fielding mementoes, which had been hastily tucked into a closet on the dawn return to the house some days before. In the haze of happiness that had been enveloping her, she and Seth had been busy swimming, loving, yachting, acquiring a wedding license, loving, sightseeing around the island, talking about future plans, holding hands, and in between times simply looking at each other and loving with their eyes. There hadn't been time to think of things like astrolabes and sextants.

Seth unpacked the box of treasures while Danny returned them to their proper places. Soon the job was done, with only the few books to be restored to the study shelves. As Seth handed them to her, Danny hunted for their time-honored niches, standing on a chair whenever the shelf was too high.

She reached downward for the last book, which went on the very top shelf, partly because it was in French and of little interest to the casual reader, and partly because it was a fragile first edition that oughtn't to be handled too frequently. It dated back to 1866, the year in which seventeen-year-old Danielle had left France to come to the New World. The slim volume was not put into Danny's hand as she had expected, and she glanced down to see that Seth was leafing carefully through it.

"Hmm. Verlaine. Interesting to look at another person's taste in literature," he remarked. "Amazing how much you can learn about someone by seeing what they underline. And the odd little comment in the margin . . . is that how you grew to understand Danielle Fielding so well?"

Over the course of several days, some of it spent in expressing her joy at the return of the Sargent portrait, Danny had revealed to Seth a good deal about her empathy for her ancestress.

"Good heavens, no. I don't speak French. Do you?"

Seth was still studying the text. "Not really, but I understand it fairly well. I crewed on French sailboats several times when I was younger, and I also studied the language in university. Here's one where she's written *'ca me touche'* . . . 'this moves me.' She wrote more, too." He translated slowly, deciphering the faded sepia ink with a little difficulty. " 'He died in autumn, and this is how I felt. I'll remember always.' "

Danny had read the comment before, and had

managed to understand most of it, for the French words were simple. "I can understand some of her remarks— it isn't hard to translate things like '*superbe*' and '*magnifique*' and '*c'est trop triste*.' But I can't understand the poetry she's commenting on, so it doesn't mean much to me."

Seth turned his attention to the poem that had evoked such deep feelings in Danielle Fielding. " '*Les sanglots longs des violons de l'automne blessent mon coeur d'une langueur monotone.*' "

"What does it mean? Something about blessing the heart?"

"No; wounding it. It doesn't translate too smoothly. 'The long violin sobs of autumn wound my heart with a monotonous languor' . . . or something to that effect."

Even in translation, there was a pervasive grief to the words, a sense of the great emptiness that had left a woman desolate on the death of her well-loved husband. And yet, because seasons change and violins create beauty, it was not a feeling without hope. It struck Danny that way, anyway; but then, she already knew that Danielle Fielding's heart had not cried forever. She had filled the emptiness with the raising of her children, and later in time with running an estate in France, and perhaps in her final years with dedication to a cause she believed in. Strange, Danny thought. After hearing that poem, I believe I understand her totally. It's as if I had cleaned the layer of darkened varnish off that old painting of her and seen the pure, strong colors beneath.

At last Seth closed the book carefully and handed it

up. "Well, she certainly picked an interesting piece to be moved by. The poem moved enough other people in its time. You do know the story of those words, don't you?"

Danny eased some books aside to make a comfortable niche for the slim volume, without looking down at Seth. "No. Should I?"

"Not necessarily, unless you've done some reading about World War Two. They were the words that started off the liberation of France in 1944. They were used on an open broadcast, readings of French poetry. When the French underground heard that particular poem, they knew the Allies were planning to land in Normandy the next day. They mobilized the whole Resistance, those words."

Danny lowered her arms without returning the book of poetry to the shelf. She stood simply looking at it, turning it over and over in her hands. "How did the words come to be chosen?" she asked.

"I haven't got a clue. Someone had a liking for Verlaine, I suppose."

With Seth's hand to help her, Danny got down off the chair. "Perhaps I won't put it away, after all," she said. "Would you mind translating a few more of her favorite poems for me?"

While Seth started to do so, Danny turned to gaze at the portrait with its faraway eyes looking eternally to the sea. Were you alive then, Danielle Fielding? Were there men in your house one dark night, talking about secret plans? Were you there? Did you, at the age of ninety-five, hear? Were your senses as sharp as ever? Did you still remember the words that had once moved you so deeply? Did you mention them to someone? And when the day came, were you once more looking out to sea?

"I wonder," Danny whispered, so quietly that Seth didn't hear her over the drone of his own voice. "I wonder . . ."

Silhouette Special Edition

MORE ROMANCE FOR
A SPECIAL WAY TO RELAX

$1.95 each

2 ☐ Hastings	21 ☐ Hastings	41 ☐ Halston	60 ☐ Thorne
3 ☐ Dixon	22 ☐ Howard	42 ☐ Drummond	61 ☐ Beckman
4 ☐ Vitek	23 ☐ Charles	43 ☐ Shaw	62 ☐ Bright
5 ☐ Converse	24 ☐ Dixon	44 ☐ Eden	63 ☐ Wallace
6 ☐ Douglass	25 ☐ Hardy	45 ☐ Charles	64 ☐ Converse
7 ☐ Stanford	26 ☐ Scott	46 ☐ Howard	65 ☐ Cates
8 ☐ Halston	27 ☐ Wisdom	47 ☐ Stephens	66 ☐ Mikels
9 ☐ Baxter	28 ☐ Ripy	48 ☐ Ferrell	67 ☐ Shaw
10 ☐ Thiels	29 ☐ Bergen	49 ☐ Hastings	68 ☐ Sinclair
11 ☐ Thornton	30 ☐ Stephens	50 ☐ Browning	69 ☐ Dalton
12 ☐ Sinclair	31 ☐ Baxter	51 ☐ Trent	70 ☐ Clare
13 ☐ Beckman	32 ☐ Douglass	52 ☐ Sinclair	71 ☐ Skillern
14 ☐ Keene	33 ☐ Palmer	53 ☐ Thomas	72 ☐ Belmont
15 ☐ James	35 ☐ James	54 ☐ Hohl	73 ☐ Taylor
16 ☐ Carr	36 ☐ Dailey	55 ☐ Stanford	74 ☐ Wisdom
17 ☐ John	37 ☐ Stanford	56 ☐ Wallace	75 ☐ John
18 ☐ Hamilton	38 ☐ John	57 ☐ Thornton	76 ☐ Ripy
19 ☐ Shaw	39 ☐ Milan	58 ☐ Douglass	77 ☐ Bergen
20 ☐ Musgrave	40 ☐ Converse	59 ☐ Roberts	78 ☐ Gladstone

$2.25 each

79 ☐ Hastings	87 ☐ Dixon	95 ☐ Doyle	103 ☐ Taylor
80 ☐ Douglass	88 ☐ Saxon	96 ☐ Baxter	104 ☐ Wallace
81 ☐ Thornton	89 ☐ Meriwether	97 ☐ Shaw	105 ☐ Sinclair
82 ☐ McKenna	90 ☐ Justin	98 ☐ Hurley	106 ☐ John
83 ☐ Major	91 ☐ Stanford	99 ☐ Dixon	107 ☐ Ross
84 ☐ Stephens	92 ☐ Hamilton	100 ☐ Roberts	108 ☐ Stephens
85 ☐ Beckman	93 ☐ Lacey	101 ☐ Bergen	109 ☐ Beckman
86 ☐ Halston	94 ☐ Barrie	102 ☐ Wallace	110 ☐ Browning